A Winter Town

by

Barb Bissonette

STRATEGIC BOOK GROUP

Strategic Book Group
P.O. Box 333
Durham CT 06422
www.StrategicBookClub.com

ISBN: 978-1-60976-739-6

Printed in the United States of America

Book Design: Bonita S. Watson

This book is dedicated to Lucas,
my beloved grandson.

Prologue

The train whistled mournfully as it pulled its weary way down
the long trail and rounded the big hill to head west. It was the *North-
land* and it would eventually truck all the way to the Rockies.

A woman and a young boy in his early teens were sitting outside and enjoying the evening after a hot, humid July day. The
woman had a striking face. When she smiled at the boy beside
her, it became almost beautiful. Her hair was caught back in a
barrette and it, too, was striking. It was pale brown, shot through
with silver—no artificial color had ever touched that head of
hair. She looked very natural and earthy.

The boy was beautiful, too without a doubt. He had huge
brown eyes and eyelashes that should never have graced the
face of a male. His looks were astounding, but at a closer range,
one could detect a note of—what? Simplicity, perhaps. Some

folks said that Skylor Barnett was just a "little slow," and that is about as apt a description as possible. He wasn't mentally handicapped, but he just wasn't right either. He could read and write, but somehow he always seemed more like a child of ten instead of a teenager of almost fifteen. The woman tried not to worry about his future, but it was hard sometimes. She loved him with all her heart and soul.

The train whistled again, and the boy shivered in spite of the warmth of the evening.

"I hate that sound. It makes me feel so lonesome."

"I know, dear."

"Do you think that it will ever stop making me feel like that?"

"I hope so, dear. I sure do hope so."

1

What a long and lonely road Highway 11, which wound mile after endless mile north of North Bay, was turning into. I had always thought of myself as a somewhat rural girl — not a country hick, but certainly an outdoorsy girl who liked to bike and hike and spend days off in the parks of the Greater Toronto Area. I didn't mind getting a little color from working outside or the odd bug bite, and I wasn't afraid of spiders and turtles and things.

This, though, was getting into territory that I was totally unfamiliar with. I couldn't imagine how much longer I'd have to drive as I passed a sign that read Marten River. I felt as if I were in a whole different world.

I was apprehensive …and trying very hard not to acknowledge my apprehension. I had a cell phone (although God only knew if I could even get a signal way up here), but still I felt cut off from the world—my world, anyways. I wondered for the thousandth time what the hell I was doing driving so far away from home to spend five weeks in No Man's Land, on what seemed to be a wild goose chase if ever there were one. Oh yes, I told myself—also for the thousandth time—it's for the money. It was all Luke's idea. I wish that Luke had taken the damned job himself and not sent me.

Luke was my brother, my only sibling, and I loved him more than life itself. Our folks were both dead, and we had only each other. We weren't mushy—not ever—but I knew that he felt the same way I did in the way that you know these things without being told. I could still be thoroughly annoyed with him, though.

We worked together, Luke and I. It was a completely bizarre business relationship, but so far it seemed to be going along not too badly. I won't say that we were thriving, because there wasn't a lot of thriving going on in the GTA these days, but we were rubbing along as well as the next guy, and there is something to be said for that.

We had hung out our shingle after Mom died. She'd owned and operated a little craft shop for years. It was halfway between Newmarket and Aurora, and it used to be out in the middle of nowhere. Now it was surrounded by other businesses and houses, since Newmarket had grown by leaps and bounds. Our mom had worked hard, and she had been reasonably successful. As Luke and I got a little older and developed our own interests, the shop became her baby. She started with folk art in the 90s, and then incorporated quilting into her repertoire. After the new millennium, she got into scrapbooking, which was the only craft that remotely interested me. She had "crop nights" and "free styling Saturdays," and she had quite a number of women who were faithful and came regularly.

It was Luke who came up with the idea of starting a business in her shop. I was all for selling it, but I truly think that Luke could not bear the thought of driving by and seeing it owned and operated by someone else. He had loved our mom dearly. It was not hard to love her. She was a wonderful mom. Our dad had died when we were both teenagers, and we held on to her as long as we could.

Mom had developed lung cancer, which was the height of injustice because she never smoked and she was a good person. We held onto her until the disease took the last ragged breath from her two years ago, when she died in Southlake Hospital on a day that I thought would end life for Luke and me. We sat by her bedside, helpless and in despair, unable to do anything for her—nothing at all, except hold her hand and whisper that we loved her with all our hearts and would love her always.

So I didn't really mind trying to eke out a business there, at that funny little shop where we'd spent so many hours helping Mom or just hanging around, waiting for her to close up and come home.

It was Luke's idea to open up a detection shop. A detection shop, mind you, not a detective agency. Luke did not want to be presumptuous. He had studied law and security in college, and I had trained as a personal support worker. I hated it. I was working in a nursing home, and I always worked nights and evenings and weekends. The patients were all incontinent and confused and combative, especially on nights with full moons. (If you don't believe that, spend one night in a nursing home when the moon is full.)

Luke had two part-time security jobs. One was at that same nursing home, and one was weekends at a plant. We were both sick of shift work. It makes you old before your time. Luke decided to keep his weekend job and quit the other. I quit at the nursing home, and we went full-throttle into business together. We were unsure at first, but we took the plunge and never really looked back. I've never been sorry, anyways. We couldn't have done it, I'm sure, without Mom's place of business available to us with no mortgage and no overhead. Still, it was a risk, and I was proud of us for taking the road "less traveled by."

We contacted one of Mom's friends, who still had some folk art paint, and she painted us a very professional-looking sign. It read:

> **Coopers Detection Agency.**
> **No job too big.**
> **No detection too small.**
> **L&G COOPER—DETECTION, INVESTIGATION,**
> **& SECURITY**

We both beamed the day that we hung it up. It looked good. It was our beacon in the world. I think that our mom would have been proud too. She always taught us that we could do anything, anything at all, if we set our minds to it.

And that's what we did. We sent out flyers. We put ads in the local phonebook and paid for an ad in the yellow pages. We set up our own website. And we got customers. I wasn't sure that we would. But we did, partly, probably, because of Mom's name; partly out of curiosity. Some of the things that people phoned about were simply ludicrous. But we turned no one away. Luke was adamant about that.

As a result, I found myself in situations that I had never dreamed of prior to our business venture. I rescued a cat from a tree. I rescued a hamster from behind some drywall—and into the arms of a very happy nine-year-old girl. I followed a sixteen-year-old boy downtown to make sure that he was not up to any mischief, which would make him unlike any sixteen-year-old boy I'd ever known.

Luke has followed a fair number of wayward husbands and two wayward wives. It made him sad, I think. It reminded him of how happy our parents had been and what a rare and wonderful thing that was. Luke also drove an elderly man miles across town twice a week to see his wife, who was in a nursing home and didn't even acknowledge him. That made him sad too. You don't realize, until you're all grown up, how lucky you have been to have had parents who not only loved you, but who also loved each other.

One dull, overcast day in October, when the leaves were fading from the trees and a damp chill had crept into our days, which were growing progressively shorter and shorter, Luke came into the store with a crooked grin on his face.

"Guess who called me last night?"

"How would I know?"

Although Luke and I spent a lot of time together because of the nature of our job, and we consulted each other on many things, we did not live in each other's pocket. We had our own apartments and our own lives. It was much easier that way.

"Take a wild guess. There's a big job in it for us."

"For the company, you mean?"

"Certainly. Biggest job we've had yet."

"How would I know?" I demanded crossly. It was too early for guessing games. I was trying to drink my first morning coffee.

Luke was unperturbed. "Sally Big Boobs."

"Who?"

"Sally Big Boobs. Don't you remember her? I used to go out with her in college, and you always called her that. Very unchristian, I might add. The girl can't help it if she's well-endowed."

"Oh ya, I remember her. A bit of an airhead, wasn't she? Or did you ever get past looking at her to investigate her mind?"

We both laughed as we remembered.

Luke shrugged. "She was all right, you know. She ended up majoring in social work and did pretty well."

"That's right. She ended up going way up north didn't she, to some fancy job? And anyways, I wasn't the only one who called her Sally Big Boobs, as I recall. I believe your friends started it. And maybe people wouldn't have noticed that she had breast issues if she wasn't always wearing low-cut tops and flaunting her cleavage about. Anyways," I continued before Luke could rise up in defense of his long-lost girlfriend, "what about Sally Big Boobs?"

"Well," Luke took a deep breath and cocked his head to look at me as if he was unsure of what my reaction would be. "She is way up north. She's up as far north as Cochrane, and then about one hundred kilometers east of that."

"Why on earth would anyone want to live way the hell up there? And what does she want us to do?" I frowned at him, apprehension creeping into my heart. "Just a minute, Luke. We don't have to go way up there do we? To do this job? I don't feel like traveling hundreds of miles. You can go, if you want to. Anyways, what kind of job is it? Isn't there anyone else living up there that could do it?"

"Would you just hold your horses, Gill? You haven't even given me a chance to tell you anything. And, of course, there are lots of people living up there. Where do you think that coffee came from?"

"What are you talking about? It came from Horny Tim's, of course." With that, I took another slug of the fine brew as I tried to follow my brother's line of conversation. I had this funny feeling that it was not going to bode well for me.

Luke smiled when I used his slang to refer to my coffee.

"Exactly! Tim Horton. He was born in Cochrane."

"He was? Are you sure? I remember going to the Tim Horton's coffee shop in Hamilton, and there was a big plaque on the wall about it being the first Tim Horton's."

"That's true. But Timmy was born in Cochrane. They finally have a Tim Horton's there too. I think they got one in 1992. A little behind, I guess."

"Just a little," I agreed dryly. "And I haven't the faintest idea what you are getting at, Luke."

"How about you keep quiet for a few minutes and listen to me, and I'll tell you what I'm getting at."

I crossed my arms across my chest and was silent.

2

So my brother explained to me about this "case." I somehow knew, right from the very beginning, that I was going to
land smack dab in the middle of it. I seemed to get the "short
end of the stick" (my mother's expression) quite often, or so
it seemed to me.

Luke had his weekend security job and so was indispensable, or so he would lead me to believe. This meant that he
couldn't possibly go—or at least he couldn't go for as long a
stretch as five weeks. Five weeks!! What was I thinking? Oh
yes, I almost forgot again. The money. Hence, it was me who
was packing, not him.

The story—as told to me by Luke—as told to him by Sally
Big Boobs— goes as follows.

There is a little village north of Timmins and east of Cochrane that is very quiet, and not too much ever happens there.
Certainly, the crime rate is very low. They've never had a murder
in all the time that anyone can remember. That is, until last year,
on the night before Halloween. "Devil's night," Lucas called it,
but I am unsure where he got that information from. Sally Big
Boobs, no doubt.

Anyways, on that night, a young boy was killed in the woods
and wasn't found until the next morning. It had snowed through
the night, which had covered up any evidence. No weapon was
ever found, and no one could come up with a motive.

"Hold the ride," I put my hand up. "Did you say 'snowed'?
In October?"

"Well, technically, it would be November, right? Halloween
is the last day of October."

"I don't care, Luke. That is too bloody early for snow in my
book. It's ...it's inhuman, that's what it is."

"Gillian Cooper, would you please focus? I'm trying to tell
you about our most exciting case yet, and you're going on about
the snow. Let me finish, will you?"

I grudgingly conceded. I did not think that it was a "most
exciting case" at all. It sounded pretty dull and mundane to me.
I think that was my problem with the whole case and how things
turned out. I never did believe, not once, in the presence of a
murderer at large in the little village of Truman Sound. I thought
the kid was probably drunk, or whatever, and stumbled in the
bush and hit his head or passed out and choked on his own vomit. Luke and I had gone to high school with someone who died
that way. But no, Luke was adamant that this kid—Ryan Mill-
wright was his name—had been murdered.

"What makes you so sure about that?" I asked. "You
didn't know him. All you're getting is hearsay from your
large-breasted friend."

"Sally is not the one who is so sure about it. Apparently,
Ryan's parents are the ones who are not satisfied with the police investigation. They said that they were very sloppy, and

they are terribly upset that nothing at all showed up in the way of evidence."

"Maybe because there was nothing to show up. What makes them think that we'll find anything a year later, when these guys are professionals?"

"They just want things looked into a little better, that's all."

Luke was being very calm and reasonable. I didn't like it. I didn't like it one little bit.

"They want people to be interviewed and questions to be asked. According to them, there is no one who would want to hurt their son. They said he was a good boy who got good grades in school. He was only sixteen."

I grunted. "Parents always think their kids are paragons of virtue. It doesn't mean that it's so."

"Still, it seems this kid wasn't a bad kid. He'd been drinking, but not very much—a couple of beers, that's my understanding. And no pot or anything. The Millwrights have a lot of money. Sally said they are millionaires, and they want his death investigated. They can afford it, and they want to hire a private detective."

"You did explain did you that we are not really private detectives, didn't you? We never had any official training."

"They know that, but anyone official probably wouldn't go so far away from …," he hesitated, "…from the city."

"They would be very wise. I don't want to go that far away either. Our cottage is far enough north for me."

Our cottage, which has been in our family since before either one of us was born, is on Lake Healy, which is just the other side of Bracebridge. It's beautiful, but it would never cross my mind to go there for a winter visit. There would be absolutely nothing to do. I suspected that was a problem with a lot of those little frozen places north of the big smoke.

"Gilly, Gilly! Where's your sense of adventure?"

"Luke, seriously, I don't want to do that. I don't care if they're rich. I don't want to be so far away from home. Why don't you go?"

"I'd love to. I really would."

I harrumphed, but he totally ignored me and went on, "But I can't leave my security job at the plant, and you know it."

"Oh, you could if you wanted to, and you know it."

"I couldn't, you know. And this would be such a great thing for us. Think how exciting it will be if you figure out what those small-time cops couldn't. It would be the making of us. And you should be able to figure it out. You've read every mystery book ever written. Some of it must have sunk into that brain of yours."

I did love mystery books, especially the old ones by Agatha Christie and P.D. James and Ruth Rendell; that much was true. I had quite a few Agatha Christies on CD and often popped one in my car if I had a long drive ahead of me. My favorite detective was Hercule Poirot, with his superior brain.

"You could use your little grey cells, like your egg headed friend, Poirot." Luke grinned at me as if he were reading my mind.

"He wasn't an egghead. His head was just egg-shaped, that's all," I said with dignity.

"I forgot how you always talk about those book people as if you really know them," Luke mused. "All the more reason for you to go and use all your knowledge."

"It really doesn't sound like much of a mystery, Luke. It sounds like an unfortunate accident."

"I agree, my dear. But if they're willing to give us two hundred dollars a day plus expenses for five weeks, who am I to argue?"

"Did I hear you right? Did you say five weeks?"

"She wants to make sure that we leave no stone unturned."

"How big is this thriving metropolis of Truman Sound? It shouldn't take five minutes to turn over every stone."

"There are a couple of hundred people there, I guess."

"A couple of hundred. Does that even qualify as a village? More like a bump in the road, I would think."

"Gilly, will you at least think about it? It would be so good for our business."

"And anyways," I went on, warming to the subject and totally ignoring his pleas, "I am absolutely, 100 percent sure and certain that Sally Big Boobs was looking for *you* to come and investigate her little millionaire family crime, not your little tagalong sister. I do believe that is how she referred to me in the past."

"Oh, come off it, Gill. That was years ago. And she said it only once."

"It doesn't matter. I'm sure she'll be on the lookout for you, dear bro, and not me."

"Well, she might," he grudgingly admitted. "But I can't go. I have my . . ."

"Weekend job," I finished for him. "I know. I know."

"It's true, you know. Will you at least think about it, Gilly? Remember what Mom used to say, 'New experiences are enlightening'?"

3

As you can guess, I did think about it, and I eventually gave in and agreed to go to Truman Sound—not very graciously, I admit. And I made Luke promise that he would come and see me at least twice, and if I truly couldn't stand it after a couple of weeks, he promised I could come home. I agreed to try and use my grey cells to the very best of my ability.

The north region of Ontario looked to be nothing but rocks and pine trees. I'd never seen so many of either one in my life. I stopped for lunch in Haileybury, on the shores of Lake Timiskaming, a decent-sized body of water almost five hundred kilometers from my house. I'd left home at seven thirty this morning. It was now almost one o'clock, and I was famished.

It had certainly been a relaxing drive, not at all like driving around at home. The highway and towns were almost deserted at this time of year. There was no shortage of transport trucks, but other than them, I felt like I was alone in the world, and very, very far from home ...or any civilization at all.

I had lunch in a little coffee shop on the main street. The people were quite friendly, and there seemed to be a lot of locals in for a bite to eat. I was surprised at how many people were speaking French. I voiced this to the lady when I was paying my bill, and she explained (as if I were just a wee bit simple) that Quebec was just across the other side of the lake and a lot of people were French or bilingual.

"I didn't realize that we were so close to Quebec," I told her. "I've never been up this way before."

"It's beautiful country," she smiled at me. "We are famous for a lot of things, our little town."

"Really?" I said, nodding politely. I had no idea what on earth a little town in the middle of nowhere could be famous for.

"We sure are. You've heard of the Montreal Canadians, the hockey team, I suppose?"

"Of course."

"Well, that team is from here. They were our home team right here in our little town in 1909, and then they left for Montreal. Two years later, they became the Montreal Canadians and ever since they've been playing in the national hockey league."

"I'm impressed," I admitted. I must remember to tell Luke. He is a Toronto Maple Leafs fan himself, but hockey is hockey.

"And, of course, you've heard of the Hardy Boys?" She was warming to her subject now.

I nodded. My dad had read the *Hardy Boys* series when he was young and had saved all of the old books. They were a little too obsolete and old-fashioned for Luke and me, but I still appreciated that they had been quite popular in their day.

"Well, the man who wrote those books, Les Mcfarlane, comes from here too. I told you, we are famous."

"Les Mcfarlane?" Somehow, that name did not sound familiar to me.

"He wrote the *Hardy Boys* under the pen name of Franklin Dixon," she explained.

I nodded. That sounded better.

"You should stop and see their boat. It's called *Sleuth*, and it's on display down by the water. There's an old streetcar and a museum to see too. We have a beautiful waterfront."

I said that I would think about it and left with her directions trailing after me. They weren't very complicated. The town was too small to need specific directions. Just turn north, and you'll find yourself at the waterfront of Lake Temiskaming. If you look across the lake, you'll see Quebec.

I thanked her for her time and walked slowly to the car. I decided to take her advice and have a little look at the water-front—not because I couldn't live without seeing it, but more to put off the inevitable remainder of my drive, which promised to be only more lonely and barren.

I was agreeably surprised. She was absolutely right. The waterfront was beautiful, even at this cold, stark time of the year. I couldn't get over the quality of the air. It was so clear and sharp that it almost hurt my lungs. I smiled to myself. I guessed that I wasn't used to the purity of this northern air—or the cold. It was at least ten degrees colder than when I had left Newmarket this morning. I felt as if I were on another planet already. Already— and I still had a couple more hours to go.

I stopped at a statue that was named "Pioneer Spirit." It was of a woman's torso, from the waist up. She had a kerchief on her head and was reaching up and holding a child, who was handed to her by a man in a cap and work clothes. Or was she passing the child to him? I couldn't tell. I moved over to read the poem that was posted beside it. It was entitled "In Each Child."

I haven't the strength to hold
For yet one moment more
An acrid haze of molten air
Shrouds the burning shore
Entire town engulfed in flame

This lake our sole flight
Praying for our God's assist
To save us through this plight
I offer you in fading stretch
This precious child of mine
Hold her safe above the waves
Reassure her all is fine
All that I have is lost to fire
I couldn't lose her too
Please bear her up a little while
Help her make it through
This town we called our home
Is now all but gone
But in each child we will find
The strength to carry on.

By Brian Beaudry

Beside it was a plaque declaring the Haileybury Fire of October 4, 1922, as one of the ten worst disasters in Canadian history. It stated that three thousand people were left homeless, eleven perished, and damages totaled over two million dollars.

I was unacquainted with any of this history, and I felt ashamed. This had happened just hours from where I had lived all of my life. I am usually a very sensible person, but I could feel the tears gather in my eyes and trickle down my cheeks as I read the heart-wrenching poem.

"Touching, isn't it?"

I turned in surprise to see a little old lady who had come up behind me completely unnoticed. She looked like an apple doll, with weathered cheeks and a little bent body. Her blue eyes, though, were bright, and she smiled warmly at me.

I thought about saying that it was the wind from the lake that was making my eyes water, but I didn't. I just nodded.

"I know, dearie. It still gets to me, that poem, every time I read it. I always think that it could have been me."

"Really?" I was too surprised to be polite, but she didn't seem to take offense. I just couldn't imagine that anyone who could have been around in 1922 was still kicking and looking so spry.

"I was just a baby, mind you. I was born in April, so I was only six months old when that fire took. I've been raised on stories about it, though. Of course, I don't remember myself, but sometimes people tell you stories over and over again and you almost feel like you do remember. Do you know what I mean, dearie?"

"Yes, I do. I'm embarrassed to say that I haven't really heard too much about this fire. The lady at the coffee shop told me there was a lot of history here, but I had no idea there would be this much."

"Oh yes, there's no shortage of that, more's the pity. This town was thriving before that fire all but destroyed us. Silver was discovered in Cobalt—little place just up the road." She gestured at my questioning look. "It was discovered in 1903, and we started booming due to all the prospectors and mine owners who moved here. Heck, there was even a street in Haileybury that was called Millionaires Row. But that all ended with the fire."

"How did the fire start?" I asked.

"Well, the summer had been a real hot, dry one." Her voice was far away, and she told the tale as if she had told it many, many times in the past. This was more interesting than any history lesson I'd had in school.

"Fire rangers had been asked to stay in the area by the residents because they were worried about that very fact—the dry summer, I mean, but they didn't get permission. I'm not sure why. It's never been properly explained, or not to me, anyways. So they left at the end of the fire season, in mid-September, and left us with no fire protection services. None at all. Well, in the fall, farmers and settlers started to set small brush fires to clear the land, as they always did. But conditions were still awful dry, and on the fourth of October, the wind turned into a hurricane and got hold of one of those little brush fires, and everything just went out of control. It destroyed 90 percent of Haileybury. Some folk went and hid in the mines, but when the fire passed over the mines, it sucked all the oxygen out of the shafts, and the people inside died. Some folk jumped into the lake to get away. You can imagine how cold that would be."

I shivered just thinking about it.

She had been very intense in her retelling of the story, but she shook her head and straightened up. "I'm sorry, dearie. I didn't mean to go on and on. Getting old, I am."

I guess you are, I thought, doing the math in my head. But I just smiled at her.

"I don't mind," I told her. "It's most interesting. And even more so to know that you were actually alive then."

She gave a little snort. "More's the pity. I'm getting far too old, for sure. I have two sisters who are both dead, and most of my friends are either dead or ga-ga. Do you know what I mean?" She tapped her index finger against the side of her head.

"Yes. Alzheimer's, do you mean?"

She gave a deep sigh. "Alzheimer's. Dementia. Old age. Whatever you call it, it boils down to the same thing in the end. So far I seem to have escaped that, at least. Sometimes I think about everything I've survived, and I always start with this fire here." She pointed to the plaque. "I always felt lucky to have a life at all when you think that this was one of the ten worst disasters in Canadian history."

"So I see. Is the lady ...I guess she's meant to be waist-deep in water ...?"

"She is, dearie."

"Well, is she handing the child to the man, or is he handing her to the woman? The poem isn't really clear. I think it could be either way."

"Indeed, it could. They say that people were passing their children on to strangers to keep them safe. It boggles the mind, it does. When I look at this statue, I always think that it could have been me. I said that before, I know." She smiled at me sideways to show that she was not ga-ga, just old. "But it does make you think."

"It does indeed," I agreed.

"My favorite story about the fire is one about a lady who had done up a whole fruit cellar full of jams and jellies, and when she saw the fire coming, she scrambled up on her roof. Every time a flame hit her house, she threw a spoonful of jam on it, and the fire finally fizzled out."

I laughed in appreciation of the story, but inwardly, I had doubts about jam alone fighting a fire of that magnitude. I kept silent though.

"The next day, it snowed. Can you imagine living through such a night and waking up to snow in the morning?"

"That would be October fifth? Is that not a little early for snow?"

"Well, you're getting to be pretty far up north here—quite a bit farther than where you're from, I'd bet money."

"And you'd be right. I'm from just outside Toronto. Sometimes we never really get any snow, just a dusting."

"I would hate that, you know. I love the seasons, every one of them. I know it gets cold up here, but I love the crisp, clean air, and I love the way the snow just makes everything so clean and bright. Snow disguises a lot of things, my dear, which you may never even discover until spring."

I was to remember these words several times over the next few weeks. I'd never realized that a blanket of snow could change circumstances so completely.

"Well, I'm a city girl, and I can live without the snow. And I must be going. I didn't realize how late it's getting."

"Would you like to stop by my house and have a cup of tea before you set out on the old highway? It would warm you up a bit. I can see you're a little chilly. What are you going to do when winter comes, child?"

Things were indeed very different here. If you were walking in a park in Newmarket and a stranger got into a conversation with you and asked you to come to her abode for a cup of tea, you'd run a mile. But this felt like just the friendliest of gestures.

I shook my head reluctantly. "I'd love to. I really would, but I haven't got enough time. I've still got a good two hours to drive, and I have a feeling that it's going to get dark early." I cast a glance at a sky that was already dark and dull-looking.

"Where are you headed, if you don't mind my asking?"

"Not at all. I'm headed to a little place called Truman Sound. It's somewhere between Cochrane and Timmins. Ever heard of it?"

"Can't say that I have, but there are a lot of wee villages that aren't on any map when you start getting up there. They're just too small. Do you have good directions?"

"I have my brother's GPS, and he programmed it for me, so I think I'll be all right."

"Visiting, are you?"

I could see the curiosity was killing her. I laughed. "It's a job, you see. My brother and I run this detection agency. We're not really private detectives or anything, but we do a lot of odd jobs and different things for people. Someone that my brother knew from school knows someone whose sixteen-year-old son was murdered a year ago, and they are dissatisfied with the investigation. No motive was ever found, nor even the smallest clue as to how it happened. They want us to look into it further—talk to the local people and so on. I don't think that I'm anywhere near qualified, but my brother does, so I'm elected, I guess. I feel more than a little nervous."

"I guess you do, dearie. A murder? Really?"

"I have serious doubts as to whether it's actually a murder or not. It doesn't sound like it to me. He was found dead out in the bush the day after he died—way up in the back of beyond."

Her response surprised me. "You know, things happen in the back of beyond, just the same as they do in the big city. People live and die and laugh and cry and love and hate—hate enough to murder."

I felt a chill go straight to my bones, and I shivered.

"It's the mother pushing for this, did you say?"

"Yes. The parents, anyways."

"I'd be listening to them then. Mothers often can sense things where their offspring are concerned—things that maybe can't be written down in black and white. But that doesn't mean they're not real."

I shrugged. "I don't have much choice. I'm committed now."

"Well, I certainly wish you a safe trip, and I hope that you are highly successful in your job. Just like Hercule Poirot."

I laughed. "I love him. I'm listening to an audio book of his right now. It keeps me going."

"I love him too. Which one are you listening to?"

"*Curtain.*"

"Oh, that one's sad. He dies in the end."

She seemed completely unaware that she may have spoiled the rest of the book for me, and I didn't have the heart to mention it.

"Anyways, look out for moose on the road. If they get in front of that little car of yours, there'll be nothing left of it. The car I mean. Those animals are huge."

"Thanks, I will. And thanks for the interesting history lesson. I really enjoyed it. And I'll never forget it." I meant it. I never did forget any of it.

I turned and waved at her as I slipped into my little Honda Fit. Somehow I knew that she would still be standing there, watching me. She was.

She returned the wave and called something after me. It wasn't until I'd shut the door that the word floated on the cold Lake Temiskaming wind into my penetration.

"Godspeed."

4

I was very thoughtful after pulling out of Haileybury and heading back to the endless pavement of Highway 11. As I stopped at the stop sign where a right turn would take me north — farther north — and a left turn would take me back to my beloved hometown, it took all I had in me to turn the wheel to the right. Sometimes I wished that Mom and Dad hadn't drilled so far into our heads about commitment and responsibility — you know, all that stuff that is considered basically overrated these days, but which Luke and I had been raised to believe in.

So I just kept going. I thought about my little eighty-nine-year-old friend whom I had just left behind in Haileybury. I had really liked her. And I'd learned a lot from her. I suppose those local people knew all that history and took it for granted, but to me, it had been fascinating. I'd always remember her, I resolved.

And when I got home, I would Google the poem that was posted there at the lake shore and print it out. I had found it very touching. I had the feeling that my mother would have liked it.

I was thinking about Mom a lot. It was probably because it was such a long, boring drive, and she tended to creep into my thoughts when they were at rest. She was never too far from my mind, and she was always in my heart. I missed my dad, of course, and I'd loved him. But my mom had been like a part of me. When she died, it was as if a part of me died too.

Mrs. Apple Doll (I never did ask her name, I realized belatedly) had been right and Poirot did indeed die at the end of *Curtain*. It made me sad because I did love Poirot, but it also left the rest of the trip for my mind to wander any which way it pleased. Good luck getting any radio channel up here between this endless line of rocks and pine trees.

I wondered what Mom would have thought about this whole expedition. She was pretty sensible and could usually see things the way they should be. She was also up for new experiences, though. It's quite likely that she may have even come up with me for a few days or a week. She always liked new places. The thought made me feel sad and miss her all over again. I wished that she were still alive and that she could be here, beside me.

I shook my head. If she were still alive, then Luke and I wouldn't have a business at all. She'd be in her craft shop, busy from morning 'til night, and I'd probably still be working at the nursing home. It's so funny how things turn out in life. I was feeling nostalgic and sentimental. I was sure it was because of that gut-wrenching statue and poem. It wasn't like me to get all emotional. I've always prided myself on being quite grounded. I pulled over to the side of the road and rummaged around for another audio book. I was relieved to find *Murder on the Orient Express*. I inserted the first disc into my CD player and proceeded to lose myself in Poirot's calamities yet again. I was glad that he wasn't dead. He was like an old, comfortable friend.

It was four o'clock when I found the proper cutoff and pulled off the main highway, and another forty minutes before I reached my destination. It was almost dark, and I'd never seen such a desolate place in my entire life. If I hadn't been weary right through to my bones, I'd have put my head down on the steering wheel and cried.

"Truman Sound. Home of one hundred and fifty souls and one Mighty Quinn."

What the hell does that mean? I asked myself aloud.

At least I didn't have to drive too far to find out where I was booked to stay for five weeks. Five weeks! *Don't think about it*, I told myself sternly. *Don't think about the number. Just take it one day at a time, like the old AA motto. One day at a time.* I knew all about that motto, not from personal experience, but through an old guy back home whom Luke and I take turns driving to AA meetings, and he's filled me in on all sorts of wisdom. I wished that I were in Newmarket right now, driving old Sam around and getting cats out of trees and making plans with my friends.

There was nothing here. No, really—nothing. A gas station. A rundown looking bar with half the letters missing. I couldn't tell the name of it, not that I cared. There was a big, dumpy-looking store with a sign boasting "Groceries and anything else you may need." There also was what looked to be some kind of a warehouse in the back corner of the store. The name of this menagerie had a sign proclaiming "The Village Idiot. Your village called—their idiot is missing." I'd never seen anything like it in my life, before or since. I didn't know what to think.

I kept driving, looking for the place I'd call home for the next thirty-five long days (*one day at a time, Gillian Cooper*), which was supposedly called Sadie's Boarding House; it was also supposedly quite respectable—that is, according to—you guessed it—Ms. Big Boobs.

It didn't take long to find it just by virtue of the sheer size (or lack thereof) of the village—one street, really. It was at the end of the street, and it looked to be in slightly less disrepair than the neighboring places of business. It was a big, old house with a large veranda and lots of windows and little decks. The main entrance was well lit, and a big sign proclaiming simply

"Sadie's" was hanging above the door. At the side of the building was a more elaborate sign that said parking was at the back and rooms could be obtained by the week or the month. It also bragged "home-cooked meals."

This was it. After almost eight hours on the road, I had reached my destination. *One thing to be grateful for*, I thought, and then I chuckled inwardly as I reflected that I sounded a little like Mrs. Apple Doll.

I took a deep breath, pulled my little car into the lot behind the house, grabbed my bag and, with a tentative knock, gingerly pushed open the big oak door. My heart was beating like a trip hammer, but I forced myself to call, "Hello."

"My, my, you must be Gillian Cooper. Are you, dear?" A short, stocky lady, who could have been anywhere from age forty to sixty, came bustling through the kitchen door, wiping her hands on the apron that was tied around her considerable waist. I hadn't seen anyone wear one of those since my old granny, and that was years ago. Her smile was broad, and her face was sunny and friendly. She gave me no time to reply as she took my free hand in both of her hands and pumped it up and down vigorously.

"My goodness, and don't you just look like you could keel right over. You must be exhausted, and that's no lie. It's a long old trip, to be sure. We've been watching for you off and on all afternoon. I'm so glad you're here safe. Come in. Come in. I've got the kettle nice and hot, and I'll make you a nice cup of tea. Or do you prefer coffee?"

She paused for a breath, and I managed to say, "Tea would be lovely, thank you."

"Have you eaten? I've got a pot of stew on the oven."

As she led me up the stairs to my room, she gave a nonstop commentary about the boarding house and its other occupants.

"Of course, it's hunting season, and we always get our fair share of hunters, so there's a lot of them coming and going just now. But they won't bother you. They get up early and go to bed early, and they might go over to the bar for a few drinks, but they're a pretty good bunch all in all. George and I wouldn't have them if they weren't. Then there's old Pete. Now don't you mind him, my dear," she turned around and nodded reassuringly at me. "He looks a little rough around the edges, does old Pete`, but he wouldn't hurt a fly, really. He used to be a miner, sure, and he got into trouble with the drink, and that's no lie. Lost his family over it. And all his money. He was quite well-off at one time is my understanding, but he drank it all away. Now he don't drink at all, but it was too late for his wife and kids. It was all just too little, too late is my guess. I can't help but feel sorry for the guy. He always pays his bills, and he likes my cooking, so he's kind of settled here. Usually he just sits and drinks coffee and reads the paper from back to front. I'm telling you this only so that you know about him. Some people find him unnerving on account of he sits and stares a lot …in between the paper readings, I mean."

Oh, sounds great, I groaned to myself.

"Really, I mean it, dearie. He wouldn't hurt a fly," she repeated, responding to my unspoken words.

We were just rounding the last step and alighting on the landing that apparently led to my room when I felt something scurrying around my ankles, and I almost fell straight back down the twisted stairs. I let out an involuntary shriek, but Sadie wasn't fazed.. She merely bent down and tousled something that was very fat and brown and furry.

"Don't be afraid, Gillian, my dear. It's just our old friend Jugs."

"Jugs?"

"Yes, George's dog."

"That's a dog!" I tried not to shriek, but my voice had a mind of its own. I think it was probably just sheer exhaustion at this point.

"Why sure, Gillian. That's Jugs. She's a cross between a Jack Russell and a Pug, so she's called a 'Jug.'"

I looked at her closely to see if she was trying to pull a poor city girl's leg, but she looked serious enough.

She grinned at me, as if she were a mind reader. "I'm not kidding. She really is called a Jug, and so George calls him the

Little Brown Jug. It always gets a laugh, and so he calls him Jugs for short. He's terribly spoiled."

I looked down at the Little Brown Jug, who did indeed appear to be spoiled, if of the criteria was his circumference. I figured that the meals probably were pretty good around here if the size of its inhabitants was anything to go by. Or maybe the dog was this big because of all the scraps that were discarded. I started to giggle. Oh dear, I was getting punchy.

Sadie joined in with a little laugh of her own. "Most people like Jugs, and that's no lie. Now here's your room. I hope you like it. We're not very fancy up here—probably very plain compared to what you're used to, I'm sure." She said this anxiously as she opened the door to a room at the end of the hall and turned the light on.

I was pleasantly rewarded. The room was a fair size, with a very comfortable-looking double bed on one side and an old-fashioned-looking dresser, with a stool and an oval mirror, on the opposite side. There was a colorful quilt adorning the bed, and towels were piled up on the stool. The pictures on the wall looked as if they were photographed locally. I could tell already, just by the scenery. They looked very fitting on the old fashioned walls-as if they had been there for centuries.

"It's a very nice, cozy-looking room," I said, looking around the large room.

Sadie looked pleased with my evident approval of my lodgings. Perhaps she had been expecting someone who was critical of her country boarding house. I had been raised in a very simple way, and I was taught to not look down on other people. Maybe she had a stereotype of Toronto people. I was again reminded of Mrs. Apple Doll and her assertion that life in the "back of beyond" was not so different from life in the city. I think she meant that everyone was alike, once a person looked past the preliminary surfaces. I felt badly that Sadie had been worrying about me, while I had been worrying about her. I felt I wanted to start again.

"I'm glad you like it, dear, and that's no lie."

I turned to her and smiled sincerely. "It would be very hard not to like such a warm, comfortable-looking place as this. I'm sorry. I'm not used to driving such a long way on my own, and I'm not used to being so far away from . . ." I caught myself from saying "civilization" and substituted "home."

She smiled broadly. "It's my pleasure to be sure, dear. I'm sorry, too, that the Little Brown Jug scared you, and it is a long way to be away from your home, and that's no lie. Do you need to call your mom and dad and tell them that you arrived safely? You're welcome to use our phone at the front desk."

I must have been tired because I could feel tears pricking at the back of my eyes, which made a total of twice for today. *There must be something in the air up here*, I surmised. I couldn't remember the last time I'd cried before today.

"My parents—they've both died."

She looked at me in horror and put a hand over her mouth. "Oh, my dear girl, I am sorry. I never thought of such a thing. You're so young."

"Yes, both of my parents died young," I explained, gratefully regaining my composure. "My dad died when I was in high school, and my mom died just a year and a half ago. I still miss her. Some days I find myself thinking that I must ask Mom about this or the other thing, and I've actually picked up the phone before I remembered that she's gone." I shrugged my shoulders casually. "I'm not quite used to it yet, I guess."

Sadie shook her head ruefully. "I guess that's one thing that you never get used to, no matter how old you are, my dear. I was forty eight-when my mom died, and there are still times I would give anything in the world just to talk to her."

Yes, I thought. *I'd love to talk to her right now.* And for no particular reason, I felt those tears trickling down my cheeks again.

"Ah, my dear," Sadie said, taking a step toward me and putting her arms around me. She felt warm and soft and sweet. "You're dead tired, and that's no lie. I don't know what your detective agency was thinking of, sending a young girl like you on such a mission, and so far away at that. Was there no one else at your office who could have come so that you could stay at home?" She asked the last question fiercely, as if she suspected them of treating me very shabbily.

I wiped my eyes and laughed shakily. Then I explained to her about my mom's shop and how Luke and I had transformed it and how this big job had come our way, and so on and so forth. I couldn't have her thinking that I was abused or anything like that. It was just that the encounters with two kind, older women in one day had made me feel so vulnerable. I was here to do a job, and when that was done, I could head home. I was pleased that she seemed to agree with me on the subject of Ryan's death, though. I had little information to go on but I was hoping that there really was no big mystery to speak of and that I could soon be on my way headed south and back home.

"That was a sad, sad day in Truman Sound, and that's no lie, but I truly don't believe that it was murder. I've lived here and close by here all my life, and we've never had so much as an assault charge. Oh, I'm not saying we're perfect, my dear. I'm not saying that at all. Far from it. We have our troubles like any other town-people overindulging and so on. But we all know each other, and we can usually deal with the little day to day problems that arise on our own. Some say it was a tramp who killed Ryan. But how on earth would a tramp find his way out here? I'm asking you. We're too far off the beaten track."

"Well, what do you think then, Sadie? Maybe you can crack the case for me now, and then I can go right back home."

She laughed. "Oh no, my dear. My mind is getting old and set in its ways, and when that happens, there's not much room for new ideas and the like. But what I think is that that poor lad slipped and fell in the bush and bashed his head on a tree stump or a rock. No shortage of either one of them around. He'd had a few drinks, so I've been told—as lads do—and the bang to his head and the fall would have knocked him cold. Then the snow came, and he lay there for too long. I can't imagine that it happened any other way."

"That's kind of what I thought too," I admitted. "But his parents certainly don't think so. I just hope that I can answer some of their questions. I can't imagine that I can discover more than the police did, but they're determined that the cops missed something, and Luke is just as determined that I'll be able to uncover some startling new information. I, on the other hand, have serious doubts."

"Well, they can afford the cost, and that's no lie," Sadie proclaimed cheerfully. "Those Mainwrights are loaded. Now, you just settle in a little and then come down to the kitchen, and I'll fix you up a nice little bite to eat. And don't worry about the meals, dear. I have instructions from the Mainwrights to feed you well. They are paying the expenses, so you might as well enjoy yourself. It's not often in life that you get such an offer, to be sure. Oh, and they left an envelope for you, dear." She pointed toward the bright quilt. "The Mainwrights, I mean." And with that, she turned to go. "See you in a bit."

I put my bag down and picked the official-looking envelope up from where it lay. I opened it and read as follows:

"Dear Gillian Cooper,
"Thank you very much for agreeing to come to this god-forsaken town and looking into the death of our son. We can no longer bear to live anywhere near Truman Sound and have grown to hate the cold and desolation of the north. We are living in Richmond Hill—not so far from your home, I guess—and both of us wish to never have to return to that horrible place again.
"Our son was a wonderful young man, Miss Cooper. He was brilliant and talented and handsome. Someone snuffed the bright light of his life out in a single blow, and I will never, ever rest until I find out who it was. The police came in briefly and did a haphazard job looking around, as they tend to do, it seems, in those remote areas. I cannot believe that he simply slipped and fell. I think that they were just too lazy or too stupid to know the difference between an accident and a homicide. Anyways, I am not satisfied, and I will never be satisfied until I have some answers.

"Sally says that you and your brother are brilliant . . ."
I groaned aloud. I had suspected all along that Sally
Big Boobs just wanted to sink her teeth, or anything
else handy, into my brother. There's no way on earth
that she would ever have called me brilliant other-
wise.
" ...and she seems to have complete confidence in both
of you. Please help us, Miss Cooper. Our son was the joy
of our lives. The world has lost a wonderful young man.
I'm not trying to tell you about your business, as I have
no experience at all in matters of this nature, but I think
that you should thoroughly question the people that live
on Singing Pines Road. It was across from that road, in
the woods, that Ryan was found, and there are about five
houses there. I find it hard to believe that no one heard
anything at all that night. I am hoping against hope that
maybe people will open up to you a little more than they
did to those pompous asses on the local police force. I
can't blame people, really, for not wanting to confide in
them. Who would?
"If you need to contact us, I have enclosed both our home
and cell phone numbers. Sadie has explicit instructions
to look after your every desire, and I'm sure that she will.
Sadie is a kind old soul. Money is no object—no object at
all. I know that you're probably thinking that it must be
nice to be able to say that . . ." (I was, actually.) "...but
I would give all the money that we have in the world to
get our son back.
"Good luck, Miss Cooper. Do your best.

"Yours sincerely,
"Barbara and Robert Mainwright."

I put the letter down and sighed. All of a sudden, I felt the
burden of this investigation weighing heavily on my shoulders.
I didn't even know where to begin, *and that's no lie.* I chuckled
aloud, using Sadie's words.

Quietly, I left the room and descended to the kitchen, which was emitting the most delectable smells of stew and homemade biscuits. This was to be my first meal of many at Sadie's, and if the smell was indicative of anything, it promised to be good.

5

When I entered the dining room, it was deserted, except for a weathered old man who looked to be about a hundred. He was occupying a dark corner near the back of the room and looking out into the black night. He wore an ancient cap, and when he saw me, he tipped it and said in a croaky voice, "Bon jour."

It sounded as if even the effort of the greeting was painful in the extreme. I nodded and smiled in return. He quickly put his head down again and concentrated on the paper in front of him.

I assumed, correctly, I found out later, that this was old Pete, and that "bon jour" was talkative for him.

The only other person about was a tall, thin man who was polishing up glasses and dishes behind the counter. He turned when he saw me and gave a friendly nod. This would be George, Sadie's husband.

Sadie came bustling out with a pot of tea and a plate of stew with a couple of biscuits on the side. I hadn't realized how hungry I really was until my stomach contracted at the mere sight of such a plateful.

She talked nonstop as she put the supper down in front of me, along with a big white napkin and a handful of cutlery. "We're not too fancy here, my dear, and that's no lie, but the food is homemade and nourishing. None of that fast food stuff that you just shove in the microwave and defrost. A disgrace, that stuff, that's what it is. A disgrace. You'll not find the likes of any of that at Sadie's, no fear of that."

"It looks delicious," I said truthfully. This was verified when I took a mouthful, and I told Sadie so. She was beaming.

"I'm so glad you like it, dear. Now, after you eat, you just leave the dishes and scoot on upstairs. You look like you're all in but the boot strings, and that's no lie. There's a shower and a tub in the bathroom off your room, so feel free to freshen up. We can have a little chat in the morning, to be sure. I can let you know the lay of the land, so to speak."

"That would be great," I admitted, starting already to perk up a little from the strong black tea and the hot, tasty stew. "I really am most unsure of where to go and even what to do, for that matter. In the letter she left, Mrs. Mainwright mentioned talking to the people who live on Singing Pines Road. I'll need directions."

Sadie laughed. "Well, it's not too hard to find your way to Singing Pines, to be sure, on account of there's only about five streets in the whole town. She wants you to talk to the folk there 'cause that's around where her poor boy died. Well, right across the street and a ways back into the bush. I doubt anyone there would know anything. But ...," she shrugged, "I guess you have to do that as part of your job?"

"I guess so. To tell you the truth, Sadie, this is all new to me too. But I'm going to try my best. That's all I can do."

"That's the spirit, my dear. And tomorrow morning, I'll tell you a little bit about most of the folk around here so you know what to expect."

"That would be great." I smiled gratefully.

She touched my shoulder with affection. "My best advice to you, my dear, is to get a good sleep and let everything sort itself out tomorrow."

That sounded like very sound advice, and without further adieu, I followed it to the letter.

6

I did sleep well under the warmth of that beautiful quilt, and I felt quite rested in the morning, as if I could tackle anything. I showered and dressed and made my way timidly into the dining room. It was a place of hustle and bustle, but it looked like it was quieting down. I glanced at the clock. It was almost nine. I must have slept in.

Sadie's smile was generous as she brought me a coffee with milk and sugar on a little tray. "You slept pretty well, did you?"

"Yes, I sure did. The bed is great. And that quilt was so nice and warm. My mother quilted—I told you about her craft shop last night—so I always appreciate the time and patience that go into making a quilt. She always said that quilts like that were made of love."

"And she would be right, for sure. You'll meet the woman who quilted that quilt very soon, if not today. Isabelle Barnett. She does a lot of crafts too. She doesn't have a store, to be sure, but she has an upstairs where she does all her quilts and so on. She lives on Singing Pines, that's why you'll meet her. She'd be one of those who Mrs. Mainwright wants you to talk to. You drink your coffee up and relax a little. Then I'll bring you some breakfast, and I'll have a cuppa with you. Most of these folk are on their way somewhere—or think they are." This last was said in an undertone to me as she winked and, flinging her tea towel over her shoulder, disappeared into the kitchen.

I did like to drink my first coffee of the day in peace, and I appreciated the opportunity to do just that as I glanced around the bright dining room. There were flowered tablecloths on the sturdy wooden tables, with plants adorning most of them. There were cheerful yellow curtains on the windows, and the whole place smelled good and wholesome and homey.

People were clearing out and yakking loudly at each other as they did so. It was plain that this was a regular spot for the locals and that for many of them, it was almost like a second home. I had seen this type of place only in old westerns. I didn't think that they existed in the modern world.

Sadie was as good as her word. She gave me fifteen minutes to savor her strong black brew and then approached me with a refill. She brought the whole pot over and pulled up another chair, as well as a mug for herself.

"Ah," she said as she poured us both a steaming drink. "There's the breakfast rush done. You might think that we don't get much business on account of it being such a small town, but there's rarely a dull moment around here, I can tell you, with only me and George—and neither of us getting any younger. Course, there's not really another place in town to have a bite, so I guess beggars can't be choosers, as they say."

"It's probably got a lot more to do with the good food than anything else. You have a lovely place here, Sadie."

Sadie blushed and looked pleased. "Sure, and I wasn't looking for a compliment, but thanks anyways."

"Well, it's the truth," I said. "I can tell already that this is a good, friendly spot. People certainly look at home here, at any rate."

I glanced around the room that held about fifteen tables. It was empty now, except for the same man in the same corner, whom I recognized from last evening. He may have not moved at all. I was sure that he was wearing the same clothes. When he saw me again, he nodded and doffed his cap with a soft-spoken "bon jour."

I nodded back and raised my hand in greeting.

"So you've met old Pete, I see," Sadie said, acknowledging our little exchange. "I told you about him last night now, didn't I? He's here just about most of the time. He always sits in the same spot. Folks just know that now—that's old Pete's spot. He doesn't ask for much, poor old soul. He's just happy to have a roof over his head. This is no part of the land to be out in the cold, and that's for sure."

"Does he live here?"

"Well, more or less, my dear. More or less. He gets a small pension, and he uses that for his room and board. He's been here about five years now. Just wandered in one day, half-frozen and half-starved to death. George took him in and helped him set up his address and stuff. He's got a soft heart, does my George. He lets Pete help him do odd chores now and then. Sometimes George will get him to do an errand or a delivery or the like. But he usually just sits by the window and watches the world go by and reads his paper. He's a good hand at the crossword, is old Pete, and sometimes he'll ask us about some word or another when there's just George and me. But usually he doesn't say too much."

Again, I marveled at the way of life up here. I couldn't imagine some homeless guy just wandering in to any place that I'd ever known and staying for five years. Why, in Newmarket there would be a mile of Social Services tape, and even then, the results wouldn't be anything like living out your tired old life in a comfy place like Sadie's—a place where the same people come in and greet you, and you don't even have to ask for a coffee or anything; it's brought to you, and all you have to do is sit and

nod in the wake of the sunny windows and read your paper. Old
Pete had surely come to the right spot to spend his old age.

"So," she said briskly, in a tone of one getting down to business. "I'll tell you the ins and outs of Truman Sound so that
when you start pounding the pavement," we both grinned at the
cliché, "you'll know who's who and what's what. It's not a very
big place, my dear, as you've probably already gathered."

"One hundred and fifty souls and one Mighty Quinn," I quoted,
remembering the sign as I drove into the village last night. "You
can start by explaining that, Sadie. Who is the Mighty Quinn?"

"Oh, that's just the old fellas' idea of a joke, that's all that
is. Our population sign got run down by an idiot on a snowmobile a few years back, and some of the old boys got together
and came up with that sign. Just for a lark, you know. Get a few
second glances."

"Oh, I thought Mighty Quinn was a real person."

"Oh, he is, dear. He is," she hastened to assure me. "Neil
Quinn is very much a real person. I know him real well on account of the fact that he and I and a few others have lived right
around here all our lives. Never wanted to leave. Always felt like
I had everything I might want right here. You know, nature and
all—the trees and the water and the wide open spaces."

I suppressed a shudder. I simply couldn't imagine.

"But Neil Quinn, well, he's a fine man, and he does a lot for
people in an everyday kind of way, if you know what I mean.
He's just a good person, is all. You can count on him. He gives
some of the high school boys errands and stuff to do so they
can make a bit of cash. He's fairly well off, is Quinn, but you'd
never know it. I'll tell you a story about Quinn that just explains
exactly what kind of man he is.

"He was driving one day in the spring, about ten years back,
and there was a big old snapping turtle crossing the road. Quinn
was afraid it might get hit by a car on account of there was a
whole slew of guys up from Timmins who were back fishing.
Anyways, Quinn stops his car and tries to hustle the turtle across
the road with a stick so he won't get hit. Because, you know,

dear, those turtles take forever and a day to cross a road at all, and those fellows from the big towns, they're always in an awful hurry, and that's no lie. Well, that turtle lashed back, and before you knew it, he'd snapped Quinn's baby finger right off."

"Oh my!" This Quinn fellow didn't sound too clever to me, but I was too polite to say so, as my newfound friend Sadie obviously thought the world of him.

"Yes, indeed. Right off. In one snap. They asked him at the hospital if he'd saved the finger in case there was a chance of sewing it back on, but of course, the turtle had made short work of that. Just a small snack for Mr. Snapper."

I looked at her closely to see if she was teasing, but she seemed serious enough. I shuddered, grateful that I had consumed only coffee so far.

"You have to watch those snappers," she proceeded cheerfully. "Anyways, Gillian, my dear, you won't have to worry about that, of course. Not on this visit, at least."

I took a gulp of coffee so that I wouldn't have to reply. Nothing on the face of God's good earth could persuade me to make another visit. Ever. This land was too cold and bleak and isolated for me. I guess that's what people like Sadie were for—to love this land. After all, somebody had to live here. And love it.

"So, enough stories for now. I'll tell you where everything is, and you can wander around as you like. When you head out the front door here, you'll want to go to the left to get over to Singing Pines Road. If you turn right, you'll just go back to where you've already come, and there's nothing there. Just a gas station and the Village Idiot—terrible name for a store, and that's no lie, but again, it's just Morgan's idea of a joke. He read it somewhere and thought it was funny, so he incorporated it into his store, so to speak. So anyways, you want to turn left and then just a few feet down, the road turns right. It really turns right only on account of the Truman River. I mean, if you go the other way, you'll end up in the river after a couple of houses. So ...," she paused for a drink while I wished desperately that I could go the other way and head straight home. "You'll pass a few more buildings. There are a couple of churches. A Roman Catholic one, which is the biggest, like they always seem to be. Then a smaller Baptist one. And in between is a little convenience store whose main purpose is the LCBO. Ironic, isn't it? It's small—just a converted old house, really, but they do a lot of business, as they do in most towns, which is a shame, I always think, and that's no lie. Just look at poor old Pete, and you'll see where the drink gets you. Nowhere."

This last was said *sotto voce* so as not to be overheard by the offending Pete.

"When you get past the second church, you can keep going to leave town—"

Oh, don't tempt me, I thought wildly.

"Or you can turn left, onto Singing Pines, and there are five families that live down that road. It goes right around the end of the Truman River, like a big letter J, and there's only one house on the other side of the river, and that belongs to Quinn, who I've already been telling you about."

As she paused for breath, George came in with two plates of toast and eggs and bacon, and he placed one in front of Sadie and one in front of me. It looked and smelled delicious. I rarely, if ever, ate a big breakfast— or any at all—so this was a rare treat. I said as much to Sadie as I reached for the utensils.

"Dear, dear," she tsked as she, too, started to eat. "Well, that's a problem you won't have around here, to be sure. We'll make sure that you eat breakfast every day. Breakfast is the most important meal of the day. Did your mother never tell you that?"

"Oh yes, she did," I laughed. "But it always seems that we're too busy."

George came out with a coffee for himself and sat down with us. "Well, you won't be too busy around here," he declared. "We'll see that you eat three squares, Sadie and I."

He smiled at me. He, like his good wife, was friendly and contented-looking. He was tall and thin and graying and appeared a little older than Sadie. They looked like the proverbial Jack Spratt and his wife, or like they should be on an ad that welcomed people to the north country.

"Has Mother been filling you in on the Truman Sound folk? Or has she just been yakking on?" He lifted his eyebrows and looked at her with a little smile.

As a rule, I don't like married men referring to their wives as "Mother," but in this case, it sounded completely natural—as if, indeed, that's what she should be called.

She took no offense to this last remark and went on, unperturbed. "I was just giving her a layout of the town, George, so she'd know what to expect, to be sure."

"She'll know what to expect as soon as she walks out the door, I would think. Town's not that bloody big that she needs a layout."

"Well, I was just saying what's what, you know. She needs to know where things are."

"And how far did you get, Sadie dear?"

Sadie paused to consider as she took a bite of her eggs. It seemed like a while back in the conversation to me too, but I spoke up.

"Sadie was telling me about Singing Pines Road, because that's where Mrs. Mainwright thought I should concentrate."

"I see. On account of that's where that poor boy died, I suppose."

"Yes, exactly."

"I might as well tell you that I think it's a bit of a wild goose chase you're on, girl," George declared.

"You don't believe the boy was killed?"

He shook his head. "I don't. I read enough detective books to know that you need a good motive, and who the hell would want to kill a sixteen-year-old boy? He was a big, strong boy too. Well, over six feet, and he played sports. He'd be able to defend himself against most people."

"What do you think happened then?" Again I felt a glimmer of hope that perhaps I could start and end my investigation right here and now. It would be great if I could wrap it up in a nice ribbon for Mrs. Mainwright, and head home before nightfall.

"I don't know. I honestly don't know," George replied simply. "I told as much to the police, and so did everyone else."

"I guess that's why she's frustrated, poor soul." Sadie sighed. "She wants answers."

"Sometimes there are no answers, Mother. People with money always think they can buy anything. Sometimes there's just nothing to buy, that's all."

7

"Then what the hell am I doing here?" I dared to ask into the silence that had lapsed on the little restaurant as we all enjoyed our plates of food.

"That's just it, my dear," Sadie rallied herself around and got down to business. "You're here to do a job, and we're here to help you," she said briskly, throwing George a reproving look.

"I was only giving my opinion. I just think that these rich people get the feeling that they're better than anyone because they've got money and that nothing can ever happen to them. It's a crying shame when a young person dies, there's no two ways about it. But things like that do happen every day. He probably choked on his own puke. He'd been drinking right? That happens all the time. Too drunk to vomit, and they choke and pass out and die. That's my opinion, for what it's worth."

"That's what I'm supposed to get, I think, is your opinion," I assured him. "I'm supposed to talk to people and find out things that maybe were missed the first time. Mrs. Mainwright just can't imagine how this happened, and no one saw or heard anything."

"Well, it's her boy, to be sure. Of course she'd want to know."

"I'm just giving my opinion is all," George repeated stubbornly.

I wasn't sure how to continue, since I didn't want to offend either one of these good, hard-working folks, but I needn't have worried. Sadie took the conversation reins and proceeded to continue our virtual tour down Singing Pines, with George interjecting along the way when the fancy took him. I just listened and tried not to calculate the cholesterol total of the breakfast that I was consuming. It was far too delicious to be healthy, I was quite sure.

"When you turn onto Singing Pines, you'll be walking along the Truman River. The houses are quite high up on account of they're built on rock that's alongside the river. Very pretty in the summer, to be sure."

"That's why it's called Truman Sound." This was from George. "Whenever you see 'sound' in a name of a place, it refers to rock formation."

I thought about this. Parry Sound and Owen Sound were the only names I had time to think of if I wanted to keep up with the two-way conversation that I was trying to follow.

"On the other side of the road is just bush. Solid bush. There's a few Ski-Doo trails through there this time of year, but otherwise, nothing. All of the houses are on the south side of the road."

"That's why they didn't find the boy right away. Who would go into that bush at all in the fall? Except, of course, the hunters, but Ryan was not a hunter. And it was after dark. It was a hunter who found him, by the way."

"Oh." I did perk my ears at that. "I don't think that I knew that."

"Oh yes," Sadie confirmed. "It was a hunter, all right. Poor fella came across him at the break of dawn the next morning, but poor Ryan was long dead by then, and it had snowed overnight."

"It was hours and hours too late to do anything by then. No wonder those folk feel badly. Not enough to lose your only son, but to think of him lying out in the bush in the cold and snow ..." George shook his grizzled head in sympathy. "You just wouldn't wish that on your worst enemy."

"The Murphys are the first family that live on Singing Pines," Sadie was bringing us back to the thread of conversation that had gotten lost somewhere along the line. "Nice family. Five kids."

"Five?" This seemed a bit excessive to me in this day and age.

"Oh yes. She's a lovely woman. Runs the local Girl Guides and Sparks and everything else put together because we're so isolated."

"Most of them are her own kids, is why," George smiled dryly.

"That's true. She's a busy one, to be sure. She really keeps thing going for the local kids. Always organizing one thing or another. She's like Mother Earth, she is."

"She's a great girl," George agreed. "Her husband's good too. Not a real ambitious sort, but a good lad."

Sadie snorted. "An Irishman."

"So?"

"All talk and very little action, if you ask me."

"We weren't."

"I was," I rushed in. "I'm supposed to ask everyone."

"Oh, he's all right." Sadie conceded. "There's no harm in him. Just not much good, is all."

"Sadie." This was in a warning tone. "You don't like him because he isn't busy every minute of the day, like her."

"True enough."

"That doesn't mean there's not good in him. You're supposed to stick to facts. He's not a real go-getter, that's all."

"You can say that again, and that's no lie. Gillian will have to draw her own opinions on all of us. Do you have to write a report?"

"I guess I'll have to," I smiled. "I better start taking notes."

They looked at each other, startled, and I laughed. I didn't honestly believe that there was one iota of harm in this whole little village—unless you included small-town values and opinions, which could be found anywhere ...even Newmarket.

"Next to Murphys live the Cathcarts. Nice couple, in their fifties, I guess. He worked for Ontario Hydro for years and then he retired early. He does those wood carvings. You may have seen them—bears and birds and so on. Really talented. They have three kids, but they all live south of here. Actually, they come from your neck of the woods."

They both looked at me expectantly, but I shook my head. I didn't know any Cathcarts. *My God*, I thought yet again, *life is very different here. They think that I will know people in a town of almost a hundred thousand people* .

"They haven't been here too long. Ten years, maybe. Nice couple."

"Then there's Claude Maindiaux."

"A Frenchman?"

"Actually, he's from Belgium."

I grinned inwardly. A Belgian. Maybe he'll crack the case for me, like my dear friend Poirot.

"Kind of a bitter old fellow," George continued. "He was a child in Belgium during the war. I think that does things to you. You see too much. You never really get over it."

"He must be a fair age then."

George and Sadie looked at each other while they considered Claude's age.

"Eighty, maybe. He's in good shape, though, and that's no lie.'

"He is that. See him out striding about on his cross-country skis, like a young fellow."

"You won't get much talk out of him. He pretty well keeps himself to himself. I don't think that half of these folk even knew Ryan. The Murphys would on account of they had kids the same age, but the Cathcarts and old Claude probably knew him only by sight. But you never know. They were all questioned at the time."

"Next to Claude are a young couple, Megan and Kyle Bloom. They have a little boy. He's only a year and a half or so."

"What do they do?"

"What do you mean?"

"Do they work around here?"

They both snorted derisively, in unison.

"Don't work anywhere. A couple of deadbeats, if ever there were."

"Don't go giving the child preconceived ideas. She's supposed to draw her own conclusions."

"You agree, Mother. You know you do."

Sadie shrugged noncommittally. "Yes, I do," she admitted. "But I'm trying to just give Gillian the facts."

"I am too. They're a couple of deadbeats. And ...," this in a more hushed tone, "I know this for a fact: they smoke a lot of twisted cigarettes."

"Twisted?"

"You know, 'wacky tobaccy.'"

"Oh, I see."

"Yes, indeed. I'm not saying that others don't, but they are a little more discreet. Those two, they just don't care who knows. Get it up at that Newfie garage is my guess."

"George, you don't know that. I thought you were just sticking to facts. Anyways, I don't care what others do. I don't, but I shudder to think of that poor baby's lungs and brain, exposed to that stuff as he is. Anyways." She hurried on as if she couldn't bear to think of the innocent in question, "At the end of the road, there's Isabelle Barnett. The one who made that quilt you like so much."

"Now there's a fine woman."

Sadie nodded in agreement. A minor miracle.

"She's a good girl."

"Girl?"

"Well, she's sixty, I guess. That's a girl, the older you get, my dear."

"She's over sixty. Didn't we have a sixtieth birthday party for her a few years ago now?"

"Yeah. You're right. Three or four maybe. I can't really remember."

"Well, Reg was alive. And he's been gone at least three."

"Reg?"

"Her husband."

"She's a widow?"

"Yes. It's sad, really. Reg and Neil Quinn were great friends, and Isabelle and Quinn's wife too. But she's been dead quite some time. She had early-onset Alzheimer's. It was the saddest thing. Quinn looked after her at home."

"Scary, when you think of it. She was only in her late fifties."

"Really? Isn't that a little too early for Alzheimer's?"

"Probably. They called it that because she withdrew. Just lied in bed for days and wouldn't get up or wash or anything."

"Sounds more like depression to me. Not ...," I hastened to add, "that I know anything about it."

"I agree with you, and that's no lie. I always said that, didn't I, George?"

"Yes, Sadie, you did."

"Because, you see, they had only one daughter, and she was killed in a car accident. Rose was never the same after that. Well, you wouldn't be, would you?"

"No, Mother, you wouldn't."

This sounded to me like a conversation that they might have had many times before.

"It's bad enough for a man, but I think for a woman, it's the end of the world."

"It was certainly the end of Rose's world."

"No other children to love. No hope of a grandchild. It just about killed her."

"It did in the end, I think. She just pined away until she died."

"Awful hard on Quinn."

"So these two couples were friends, and they both lost their partners?" I asked. I was getting a little lost again.

"To be sure. We were talking about Isabelle." Sadie remarked.

"Yes. And you both agreed that she was a lovely woman." I smiled, but they saw no irony in this.

"Well, like I said, she lives at the end of Singing Pines, before it goes around the bend of the river, which is just huge rocks, and then there's Quinn's house. So they live across from each other, really, but of course, they're separated by the water."

"So they're both alone now?"

"Well, Quinn lives alone, but Isabelle is raising her grandson."

"Oh really? How old is he?"

Again they looked at each other in concentration.

"Fifteen," they said in unison.

"A nice boy, but not quite right, if you know what I mean."

"He's mentally challenged?"

"No-o-o. Not exactly. Nothing as bad as that. He's just . . ."

"He's damaged, is what he is, dear." Sadie concluded with conviction.

"Damaged? By what?"

Again, they looked at each other, as if undecided what information they should divulge to a girl of such short acquaintance.

Sadie sighed and launched into the topic, which seemed to be a delicate one.

"You see, Gillian dear, Isabelle and Reg had two kids. A boy and a girl. The boy made out okay. He lives down in North Carolina and has a good job as a computer analyst. Just whatever that is, I am most unsure, but I'm told it's a good job. But," she sighed again as she seemed to be coming to the unpleasant part of the family fable, "Shantelle, her daughter, didn't make out quite so well."

"She died?"

"Might as well have," George proclaimed grimly.

"What happened to her?"

"Well, my dear, she got in with the wrong crowd. It's an old, old story that's often told, and it's a real shame, is what it is. Beautiful girl she was too."

"And a nice girl."

"Oh my, yes. She was like a wee ray of sunshine, that one. Right up until she was about fifteen. Same age as Skylor is now. Funny, when you think of it that way, isn't it?"

"Skylor?"

"That would be Shantelle's boy, to be sure."

"Oh, I see. Isabelle Barnett is raising her daughter's son, and his name is Skylor."

"Of course, dear." Sadie looked at me as if I, too, might be a little slow on the uptake. "That's it exactly."

"Where is Shantelle?"

Sadie and George shook their heads and shrugged.

"Nobody really knows. Out west somewhere."

"Vancouver Island is my guess. They say there's a powerful lot of drugs out there."

"So nobody knows where she is?"

"She'd be one of those people that you hear about with 'no fixed address.'"

"Oh my goodness. How very sad. How old is she? A lot of kids get into drugs, but they straighten out when they start to grow up a bit."

"That's true, dear. But some of them just get stuck in that spot and can't get out, and they get lost. Shantelle would be thirty-one now, because she was sixteen when she had Skylor. It just about tore the heart right out of Isabelle. You see, Shantelle just left without a word. Reg and Isabelle didn't even know that she was pregnant. They didn't hear from her for two whole years. Then she called and told them that she was with some guy and she'd had a baby boy who was already a year old. Isabelle loves kids, and she wanted to go out and see them, but Shantelle wouldn't tell her where she was or the name of the guy she was with. Remember how thin she got then, George?"

"Very sad," George agreed. "For both of them. It was like they aged overnight. But they were very open about it all—both of them. They told everyone in town in case someone heard anything, anything at all. Isabelle used to say that she just wanted to see the little guy, that she couldn't bear the fact that there was a boy in the world who was part of her and Reg and she couldn't know him. All she knew was his name. Skylor Reginald Barnett."

"Named after his grandpa. That's nice," I ventured. "Isn't it?"

"Oh yes. Anyways, it was another two years before they heard from Shantelle again, and she was in real bad shape by this time. She was far gone into the drugs, and Children's Aide was going to take Skylor. He was three and not being properly looked after. I think they were living in their old car, which didn't even run. I guess that's why so many junkies go out there, because it's warm enough to do that. Up here, you'd freeze to death, for sure."

I nodded. Even in the GTA, it gets too cold in the winter months to live in a vehicle, especially with a child. I shuddered at the thought.

Sadie nodded in understanding. "I know. It's hard to bear thinking about, isn't it?"

"Anyways, Reg and Quinn flew out and brought him to Truman Sound, and that's where he's been ever since."

"Reg and Quinn?"

"Yes. They wouldn't let Isabelle go. She was to stay home and get things ready for the wee lad. I think the men thought they were protecting Isabelle by leaving her here, but she is far from a stupid woman. She knows the lay of the land. Anyways, she did indeed get everything ready for that boy, and he's been her whole life ever since. George and I were at her house helping her when Quinn and Reg arrived with Skylor, and I will never forget the look on her face."

"Nor will I," George agreed solemnly.

"She fell down on her knees, right there in the snowbank, and she put out her arms. And I tell you, Gillian, that child went right into them as if he'd known her all his little life. He was only three years old. But I guess even a child that age knows love when he sees it."

"She sure loves him," George declared. "He's a lucky little lad to end up with them. He's the only thing that got Izzy through when Reg died."

"My goodness," I observed. "This lady has had a very sad life."

"Yes, in some ways, I guess. But Reg and Isabelle had Skylor for ten years or so, and they were happy as anything. They used to take that kid everywhere, and they always had a good time. Skylor is a lucky boy, really. If he'd been put into care with the Children's Aide, he would have been bounced from pillar to post, and God only knows where he would have ended up."

"So his mother never sees him?"

"No. They never heard from Shantelle again. Not to my knowledge, anyways. I think it's at the point now where Isabelle just wants peace and to raise Skylor on her own."

"Well, how is he damaged?"

"I guess that's not really the right word. Delicate is more like it. I mean, he does all right in school and everything. It's more as if he's childlike, you know. He seems younger than fifteen."

"Yes, he does. He seems like a kid, really. He hangs around with the Murphys, and they're all younger than him."

"Not all of them, George. But it's true, he does seem kind of left behind in the maturity department. We used to think it was because of the drugs his mother took."

"Did she take them when she was pregnant?"

"Of course, we'll never know, but I would think it's quite likely."

"So some of his social slowness could be due to that," I observed.

"You're probably right, my dear. Anyways, you'll meet him yourself if you're over that way."

This made me think that I should get on my way and try to digest some of the information that I had received this morning. I should, at least, try to act like a professional, even if I didn't feel like one.

I stood up and thanked George and Sadie for the great breakfast and for the information to get me started on my quest.

They waved away my thanks with assurances that all meals were included in my stay and with good wishes on the day that lay ahead.

They were sure that I could walk everywhere that I wanted to get, and they said I could leave my car at their place, but I felt the need to look after my little Fit after her long journey yesterday. I was out of windshield washer fluid and my gas light was on, so I took her down to the gas station that I had noticed last night on my way into town.

Gas was certainly more expensive here, I noted as I filled up. I was glad that I could walk everywhere, even though my little Honda was most economical. I was fiddling with the hood so that I could replenish my windshield washer fluid when a fellow came strolling out of the garage, giving me a quizzical look.

"What's up?"

"I can't get my hood up," I explained with a rueful sigh.

"Sure, and why don't you do like he does," indicating with his thumb the other fellow who was emerging from the gas station. "And put a hat on."

"A hat?"

"If you can't get your hood up …," he chuckled.

As I gazed at the other fellow, I saw the sign that hung above the door.

"A couple of Newfs at your service," it read.

So this is Truman Sound, I thought. *Here I am.*

8

Just as I was finished with my car and settling up with these two self proclaimed "newfs," [aka Newfoundlanders] a big, shaggy, old black dog came and tried to get right in my car.

"Your dog seems to want to come with me," I observed wryly.

"Oh, he's not our dog."

"He's not? But he came out of your garage."

"Well, you see, last night it was our turn to have him sleep over and he's just getting up. Lazy old thing." The man rubbed the dog's neck affectionately.

"His turn?"

"Ya. He takes turns, does Truman."

"Truman. Is that his name?"

"Sure. He belongs to the whole town now, don't he? He's a stray that adopted us about six years ago. Kind of like *The Littlest Hobo*. Do you remember that show?"

I shook my head.

"No, I guess not. She'd be far too young, Shane," the second man said in a rebuking tone.

"I suppose it was a while ago now, that show," agreed Shane, unperturbed. "Good show, actually—a lot better than some of the garbage that's on TV these days."

He turned to me and explained, "It was about a German Shepherd who wandered around, from town to town, and did a lot of good deeds on the way. He'd help people in danger and catch robbers and stuff like that. Not that our old Truman's very smart," he added, scratching the dog's ears. "Maybe he did good deeds when he was younger and just decided to retire to Truman Sound. Anyways, we all look after him. He's better looked-after than lots of folks, is Truman. He never misses a meal, that's for sure."

"So it's okay if he comes with me?"

"Oh sure, girl, and can't he go just wherever he wants, now. There's no rules in this little place. You'd be the girl from down Toronto-way that's looking into young Ryan's death, I suppose."

"I am. Sorry, I should have introduced myself. My name is Gillian Cooper."

The man stuck out a grimy hand and shook mine in a very friendly manner. "I'm Ian, and this is Shane. Two newfs at your service."

They both laughed and I joined in. I got the feeling that this was an introduction that they had used many times over the years.

"Crying shame about that boy, and that's the truth," Shane shook his head in a sorrowful manner. "It's always sad when a young person dies, I think."

"Did you know Ryan?"

"A little. He was okay, really. A bit full of himself, but that's not unusual in a lad that age, especially when he's as big and good-looking and athletic as he was."

"And rich."

"True enough. Most folks around here have just enough to get by. Not a lot of wealth in any of these isolated towns. People stay because they want to. But the Mainwrights were loaded—

millionaires, I heard. He was up here for just a couple of years to do a research project or something with the pulp mill."

"How come he was so rich?"

"Oh, it was all in the family. Actually, I think it was her family that had the money. Her father was big into Hershey's chocolate, or something like that. He seemed like an ordinary Joe, really. But she thought she was high society. I don't know if you've noticed, but there's no real high society around here."

I admitted that I had, but I hastened to add that everyone I had met was very friendly indeed.

"Well, you're staying at Sadie's, and she and George are two of the best. You'll find that most folks around here are pretty good. It's kind of a kick in the teeth to think that Mrs. Mainwright thinks one of us deliberately killed her kid. I just don't know why she'd think that anyone would want to. That's what I can't understand. He was just a kid, for Pete's sake."

"I'm not sure if that's what she thinks," I tried to explain. "I think that she just thinks there's more to it than we know, and she wonders if anyone knows something that they might tell me, but maybe not the police."

They both shrugged.

"Well good luck to you. We'll likely see you around. If you have any troubles with your little car, bring it over."

I slid into the driver's seat. Truman was sitting patiently in the passenger seat, acting as if he had known me all my life. He looked at me expectantly.

"We're not going far," I told him, "just down the street."

He jumped out when I parked behind Sadie's and trotted over to the back door. I saw George open the door and let him in. Truman must have had a dog dish there, because he was bent over, wolfing something down, probably trying to consume it before that fat jug dog came to claim it.

I sighed and set out on foot to scout out Truman Sound. It was a very lonely feeling to be walking in a strange town on a winter afternoon. I felt isolated and homesick, and I was very, very annoyed at Luke. It would be so much easier for a man to

do this. Girls were not made to be wrenched out of their sur-
roundings and transplanted so many miles away for such a long
length of time.

I followed Sadie's directions and turned right at the end of
her road, which took me past the churches and the little store
featuring the logo LCBO that was betwixt and between them.

"I'll be visiting you later," I said to the LCBO sign as I
walked past it. Saturday night in Truman Sound. What the hell
else would I do to stave off my loneliness?

I turned left onto Singing Pines. It really was beautiful. The
houses lined the south side of the road, but the north side was
all pines. The snow was deep, and it was adorning the trees like
a bright, shimmering mantle, with the sun streaming through
the branches. It looked exactly like a Christmas card. When the
wind blew, it made the snow dance and shine in the sunshine,
like daytime ghosts.

The first house was a rambling, old-fashioned, two-story
house that looked very homey.

There was a basketball hoop pinned up on a tree to the side,
and a plethora of toboggans and flying saucers, facing every
which way, flanked a hill that spread down the other side of the
house. I didn't see anyone outside in the front yard, but I heard
the racket of kids from behind the house.

There was a wooden sign hanging from a tree just off the
main road to announce this house. Carved into it was a little
elf or gnome, or some such a being, which was blue in color
and sporting a green hat. "The Murfs," was carved beneath it.
Underneath "The Murfs" was listed what I assumed were the
family members' names: Willie & Ale, Camille, Kieran, Fiona,
Sean, Shay. Oh, now I got it. It was supposed to be a Smurf.
But didn't they wear white hats? I thought so, except for Papa
Smurf; he wore a red hat, I think.

I remembered that Sadie had told me that these people were
named Murphy. Willie and Ale? What kind of names were
those? How could you determine which was the man and which
the woman? I recalled the conversation about the mom who led

the Girl Guides and other groups and the dad who was an Irishman. Maybe that explained the green Smurf hat. But which was
which? *Now there*, I thought, *was a mystery.*

The houses were not too close together. There was lots of
room between them. I wondered what it would be like to live in
a place with so much land and space. It would take some getting
used to, I concluded.

The next house was a modest ranch, which was very trim
and neat—nothing like the rough and tumble of the Murphys'.
This must belong to the Cathcarts, who had moved up from my
"neck of the woods." She had told me about his tree carvings.
To serve witness to this fact, on the front lawn I beheld a large,
carved wooden bear sporting a welcome sign. He was most impressive. Mr. Cathcart was evidently good at his work.

The next house was very small and looked a little neglected,
though I couldn't say exactly why. It didn't seem liked there was
too much life around here. This must be where the Belgian, who
was over eighty, lived. No one was in sight.

The next house looked neglected as well, but in a different
sort of way somehow. It seemed like no one really bothered with
it. There was a stroller sitting out on the porch, suspended in the
snow, and the driveway appeared to have been shoveled in a very
haphazard way, as if only the bare minimum was done. A sign was
perched on a tree overhanging the driveway. It read "Megan &
Kyle Bloom." There was no mention of a child, but at least I could
easily tell who the husband was and who the wife was.

These were the pot smokers, according to Sadie and George.
They weren't overly fond of either of them, it seemed.

There was a walk, a few hundred feet long and lined with
some trees and rocks, and then I came to the last house on the
left. It was a log cabin with a green metal roof. There was smoke
billowing out of the chimney, and the whole place looked warm
and inviting. An assortment of bird feeders adorned the front
lawn, and birds of all colors and sizes were feasting at them. At
the end of the driveway was a pole with four birdhouses strung
across it. They were all brightly painted—red and yellow and

green and blue. On the other side of the driveway was a large inukshuk-that symbol of Canada that was popping up more and more along the roads. It was a hodge podge of smooth rocks piled together to make the statue of a person. They were supposed to indicate a "welcome" to those who passed by. This one had a black hat perched on it, as well as what must have been peanut butter smeared all around it. I say this because there were birds swarming all over it too.

This must be Isabelle Barnett's, I surmised, and she must like birds. I was a detective after all.

I didn't see anyone around. In fact, I hadn't seen anyone at all at any of the five houses I'd passed so far—just heard the sound of kids at the Murphys'. *Just as well*, I thought. I didn't feel like meeting anyone yet. Everyone so far seemed to think that there was no hint of anything "fishy" in regard to Ryan Mainwright's death. It seemed to be viewed as an unfortunate accident. It didn't help that I, too, held this opinion, as did Luke, I was quite sure, if he would only be honest with me. I felt like an unwelcome intruder.

I followed the road around the bend of what George had identified as the Truman River. There was just one house on the other side of the river, which Sadie had said was Mr. Quinn's. It was a very nice house, two-story and elegant, sitting directly across the river from Barnetts'. They had been good friends when their spouse had been alive, I'd been told. It was all kind of a sad story—people dying young and babies left to be raised out here at the back of beyond.

A man was doing something on the porch with a hammer. He looked to be in his sixties, but was still powerfully built and swinging his tool with great strength. This was quite a handsome man, with a mane of white hair and friendly features ...and missing a finger, I remembered.

When he looked up and saw me, he waved and smiled and resumed his job. I waved back and turned around to retrace my steps down Singing Pines.

9

I walked back to the boarding house with a heavy heart. It was late Saturday afternoon. If I were at home, I'd be getting together with some friends, and we'd be going out somewhere. If we weren't going out, we'd be hanging out at somebody's place, with a keg of beer and a couple of movies. And maybe some Chinese food or a pizza—all those things that are inherent to Saturdays. Maybe Luke and a few of his guy friends would come along too, and we'd play euchre or something. I felt completely and utterly alone. I sidled in the back door of the boarding house, slipped up the stairs, and cried on that beautiful quilt out of sheer self-pity, not to mention homesickness. I was miserable. I know this was silly for a grown woman but it was so isolated up here and I was so very far from home.

I was amazed to discover, an hour later, that I had actually cried myself to sleep, just like a child. I sat up and rubbed my eyes. It was starting to get dark already. I looked at the big red numbers of my clock radio. It was only four thirty. I moaned.

Then, because I was a child of my parents, who had been the most down-to-earth and sensible people in the world, I sat up and, with an effort, pulled myself together. I had promised Luke that I would try, and try I would.

I pulled on my coat, hat, mitts, and boots and applied Chap-Stick to my lips. I remembered an old interview with Shania Twain in which she had said that growing up in Timmins, her ChapStick was something that she couldn't do without.

I was surprised to find the air so cold and still. It seemed to get dark early in this little place. I didn't know which way to head. I even thought of climbing in my little car and taking it for a spin. But fear of the unknown roads and getting lost held me back. I ended up turning to the right at the end of my road, with some vague visions of a six-pack of beer, only to find that the little store between the two churches was closed.

The inside of the Catholic Church was lit up, and the effect was quite stunning. The stained glass windows shone like beacons on the white glow of the snow outside and fell to rest on a wooden nativity in the yard. There was a sign posted, with a notice on it proclaiming "Five o'clock mass here. Every other Saturday."

I smiled inwardly. I guess if you lived here, you would know which Saturday was "every other." I assumed that not many people were just wandering through town, like I was.

I also assumed that this must be the Saturday for them to have mass because I saw the doors open and a few people straggle in.

I had been raised a Catholic, and as children, we had always gone to mass, with Mom more than Dad. Mom sang in the choir, and I used to love to listen to her sing. Dad was what my mother had called a "C & E" Catholic— a "Christmas and Easter Catholic." My dad had been a good-living man, though, and my mom had always pointed out that this was the most important thing, which I still believe.

Since Mom died, Luke and I have both seriously lapsed in our mass attendance—even at Christmas and Easter. I suppose the last time that I had actually been inside a church at all had been at Mom's funeral. It always gave Mom so much pleasure when we went to church with her. There just didn't seem much point anymore.

But tonight was bitter cold and I was desperately lonesome, and the truth was that I had nothing else to do at that moment, so I slowly climbed the snowy steps, opened the heavy, ornate door, and stepped inside. The air was warm and welcoming. I blessed myself and slid silently into one of the old wooden benches.

The good thing about being a Catholic was that you could go into any Catholic church and know what to do—when to kneel and when to pray and when to offer "peace" to others.

I could see people looking at me with curiosity. I guess that is only natural in such a tiny town. There were only about twenty people. The choir consisted of two women, and there was no organ in sight. Two rows from the front was a couple with their five children between them. *The Murphys*, I surmised. *But which of you is Willie and which is Ale?* I heard the smallest boy say to his mom in a stage whisper, "Who's that, Mama?"

Mrs. Murphy (I assumed) shushed him gently and smiled at me apologetically. I smiled back to show that there were no hard feelings. Actually, it was kind of nice to be among people and feel a part of things, even in a small way. I shook all seven of the Murphys' hands at the sign of the peace.

Maybe if I was friendly, they would open up to me. I could spend some time with the entire Singing Pines crowd, pick their respective brains, and get out of this desolate town as soon as possible. It was the first cheerful thought today.

One of the women from the choir stood up and made her way to the front of the church. She stood in the light of a stained glass window, which displayed Mary Magdalene, and read "Because you have loved much, much is forgiven." She was not young, but her face was very striking. Her hair was long and light brown, with a lot of grey, and it was braided so that it fell down her back. Her face was serious, but very gentle. She looked at the little congregation and smiled a little shyly.

Then she sang. She just opened her mouth and sang. She had the voice of an angel. There was no organ and no accompaniment, and there was no other sound in that big, dimly lit church except her magnificent voice. She sang "Ava Maria."

I mentioned that my mom had been a part of our church choir. She'd had a beautiful voice, and I had never tired of listening to her sing—in church, at home, or at recitals or concerts. Ava Maria had been one of her favorite songs, and I'd never heard anyone else sing it. She used to say that it was a way of talking to Jesus without prayer, that the song was a prayer in itself.

I was totally unconscious of the tears streaming from my eyes until I discovered that my cheeks were wet. Even then, I didn't care. I hadn't felt so close to my mom since she died. Here I was, in this isolated church, miles and miles from anyone I knew, and I was moved beyond my own soul. I closed my eyes and felt, rather than heard, the song soar straight through me.

You are my heaven on earth
You are my last, my first
And then I hear this voice inside
Ava Maria, Ava Maria."

At these last words, the hush inside the church was deafening. Even the Murphy children were all silent. I stayed seated on the bench after the service ended. I wanted to savor the feeling of wonder that I had found—that I had missed for as long as I had missed my mother.

It was the woman whom I had taken for Mrs. Murphy who approached me. She stopped and smiled at me in a friendly fashion, paying no heed to the two children who were tugging at her arms, each in an opposite direction.

"I'm Willie Murphy," she pulled her hand away from the child on her right and thrust it out to me. "You must be Gillian."

I took her hand and smiled back. I was self-conscious about the remnants of tears, which I hastily dashed from my cheeks and admitted that I was.

"It's a beautiful song, isn't it?" Her tone was very gentle.

"Yes. My mother used to sing it, and I have always loved it," I said by way of explanation for my emotion. "It's a wonderful song."

"I quite agree. It's very moving. And Isabelle has the voice of an angel."

"Isabelle?"

"That's who sang it. Isabelle Barnett. Have you met anyone yet?"

"Not really. Only Sadie and George. Oh, and the two Newfs at the garage."

Willie Murphy laughed.

"That's what they called themselves," I hastened to explain. "I wasn't making fun of them."

"I didn't think you were. We all call them that, except for my husband. He calls them Pete and Repeat."

I laughed. That had been a saying of my fathers. This whole town felt like something familiar. It was a good feeling.

She stuck her arm in mine and guided me down the aisle. "Since you don't know anyone, why don't you come and spend a bit of time with us? On Saturday evenings, we all usually have a get-together down by the river. We have a bonfire and roast chestnuts and weenies, and the kids skate. My husband has kind of a wine-making business, not like a bootlegger or anything. It's all legitimate. I'm sure you've seen those wine-making stores. Well, it's just the same, but Ale does it in our basement. It's so expensive to buy at the LCBO, and folks like a little pull of something on these cold winter nights."

I laughed and admitted that I, too, appreciated a little "pull" now and then and that yes, it was very cold up here.

"You get used to it, you know. But I'm sure that it's quite different than down Toronto-way."

We were outside now, and the air was so cold that it hurt to breathe. The night was clear and crisp and the stars were breathtaking. At Willie's suggestion, I fell into step with her and her clan as they made their way up Singing Pines.

She was one of the friendliest, nicest-natured women I have ever met—before or since. It seemed as if she scooped me up out of my sad, homesick mood and deposited me in a warm place. She chattered as we walked along, explaining who everyone on the street was and where they lived. I was wise enough not to mention that I knew about a lot of the people already. Besides, everyone has her own slant on things.

At least I figured out the names. Her name was Wilhelmina, which was shortened to Willie.

"It's an awful name, isn't it? I hated my name when I was growing up. My folks were Dutch, and Wilhelmina was a queen. They thought I should be honored to be named for royalty, but I always hated my name. I used to get called Nelson when I was in high school. Kids are cruel, as I'm sure you know."

"Why Nelson?"

"Well, for Willie Nelson, of course."

"Oh, I see. Why didn't you go by your second name then? I have a friend who didn't like her first name, so she started going by her middle name in high school."

"Well, Gillian dear—Gillian is a lovely name, by the way, and I'd have died to have it for a name—because my middle name is Matilda."

"I see."

"Anyways, my friends eventually just started to call me Willie, and it stuck. Of course, my parents didn't like it. They were very old-fashioned. My father said that Willie was bastardizing a beautiful name. But at least I could live with it. Sometimes, though, people see our names written and don't know which is which."

I laughed appreciatively. "I can see why. Your husband has an unusual name too. Is it short for something?"

"No. It's really more of a family nickname. His real name is Brian, but I'll tell you right now, if you were to ask for Brian

Murphy, no one would have a clue whom you were referring to. There's been an Ale in the Murphy family for generations."

She continued to babble on in a very friendly fashion, and I found myself swept into the Saturday evening festivities of Truman Sound. I guess in a town of this size, in the middle of the dead and white of winter (and this was only November), you had to make your own good times and fun. If you didn't, it would be just plain desperate, that's all.

We stopped at the Murphys' house for supplies, which Willie had all ready in boxes to be transported down to the party site. She was a very organized woman, but I suppose a mother of five would have to be. I couldn't imagine it. It sounded like a type of purgatory to me. But Willie was a warm, happy soul. Her house was topsy-turvy and very lived-in. There were crafts covering the long wooden kitchen table, from one end to the other. They were for the Girl Guides, she explained. There was a fruit bowl on the counter, with bananas, writing on their skins, spilling out of it. I was looking at them quizzically when she caught my gaze and told me with a smile that the scribbles were her children's names.

"So no one gets away with taking one too many—or doesn't get one."

She shifted the box on her hip in an expert fashion, waving away my offers of assistance, and we set off down the road with the five "Murfs" in tow and Ale bringing up the rear, a huge box full of wine bottles cradled in his arms.

Our destination turned out to be the log cabin with all the bird feeders and houses. Down closer to the river there was a bonfire, and white and blue lantern lights were strung along from the house to the river bank. The night was as clear and cold and bright as a living being. It seemed to have an entire life of its own and was like nothing I had ever experienced before. I thought that it was incredible, although I had a genuine fear of freezing—or at the least, getting frostbite in my extremities.

It was nice to be with Willie because she just inserted me into the Singing Pines crowd as if it was the most natural thing ever. I suppose that they must have heard that I was coming, and I wondered if they might resent me, but I didn't sense any animosity at all.

I felt sure that it was because there was nothing to hide and that I was going to come up with a big, fat, blank report for Barbara Mainwright. At any rate, I appreciated the ease and friendliness with which they accepted me into their little gathering.

It wasn't just the people living on this road who were partying, but also several families from the houses "in town." All told, there were about a dozen kids skating and hooting on the frozen river. They had nets up and were playing a semblance of hockey. Others were playing crack the whip. I had no idea that people still played that game. I felt as if I had stepped back in time. And I felt badly that I hadn't brought anything to contribute to the potluck, as the party seemed to be a combined effort of the conglomeration of people standing about the fire. Willie waved away my concerns and assured me that I was there as her guest and that they had brought plenty.

"Anyways, there's always tons of food. You can bring something next time, if you like."

I felt disproportionately pleased that she thought I would be able to come again and accepted the glass of white wine that she thrust into my mittened hand before she hastened to pull who must have been her oldest boy—Kieran?—from the clutches of what may have been the beginning rumblings of an altercation.

The woman who had sung at the church I already knew to be Isabelle Barnett. She strolled over to me and started to converse in a pleasant manner. It was the same thing all over again—who I was and why I was here, but I didn't mind. After all that, was my purpose.

I told her how much I had loved her solo and how special that song was to me. "I've never heard anyone except my mom sing it. You did an absolutely beautiful job."

"Yes, it's one of my favorites too. I always remember my mom saying what a masterpiece it was when Barbara Ann Scott skated to it at the 1948 Olympics in Switzerland—that she looked just like an angel. She won a gold medal, you know.

They actually named my sister Barbara Ann. There are a lot of Barbara Anns who were born in the early fifties. I don't imagine you even know the name. You don't hear too much of her anymore."

I grinned. "Actually, I do. My mom told me that story—the exact one that you just did."

"I'm glad to hear that. It's nice to know about things like that. I tried to pass these things on too. She has to be eighty by now."

"Mom told me lots of things like that—me and my brother. There were just the two of us. Both of my parents are dead now. I loved my dad, but I miss my mom a lot more. Sometimes I think that I'd give anything if I could talk to her just one more time."

"What would you say?"

The question was a little unexpected. I had to laugh as I admitted, "Oh, nothing really important. You know, just everyday stuff. She used to always ask what was new, and I knew that she really meant it. You don't appreciate that when you're young. You don't realize that most people don't really give a shit how you are."

The words had slipped out unconsciously, but Isabelle Barnett just grinned.

"You're right Gillian. No one loves you like your mom. It's a cliché, but like most clichés, it's quite true."

"For some reason, I've been thinking about her a lot. It's funny, I can go for ages and ages and not miss her too much, but then there are times, like the last few days, when I find myself longing for her."

"Probably because you're so far from home," she said sympathetically. "How long are they going to make you stay with us? Do you have to go home with a solution or a suspect or something?"

"I don't know," I admitted woefully. "It's my brother's fault, really. He used to go out with this girl, and she's a social worker somewhere up here now, and she somehow knows the Mainwrights. Luke thought it would be so good for the business to take on this job. We're not proper detectives, he and I, and the Mainwrights know that. But anyways," I shrugged, "here I am."

"Well, you might as well have a good time while you're do-ing your detection work. It's really quite beautiful up here. God's country, they call it. I know that it probably doesn't seem that way to someone from the city, but I wouldn't live anywhere else myself. I've got everything that I need right here."

It was an echo of Sadie's words, and I was amazed. This north country must put a spell on you, or something.

My thoughts were interrupted by a boy of about fifteen who came over to Isabelle and slipped under her arm. He was almost as tall as she was, and his features were breathtakingly beautiful. His lashes were long and dark, and his eyes were blue and bright.

"Nanabelle?"

"Yes, dear."

"Can I go into Cochrane next Wednesday with the Murfs to watch a hockey game? There's a good one on at the Tim Horton Center."

"We'll see. Skylor, this is Gillian Cooper. She's going to be up in Truman for a few weeks. Gillian, this is my grandson, Skylor."

Skylor held out his hand and mumbled that he was pleased to meet me. I returned the sentiment and then told him I liked his version of the name Isabelle.

He smiled at me and then ran off to tell Fiona Murphy, in our hearing, that he would "most probably" be able to accompany her to Cochrane.

"I get called everything. Skylor always calls me Nanabelle. It's his idea of a chuckle. Folks around here call me Belle or Izzy."

"How old is Skylor?"

"He's fifteen. He'll be sixteen in March. I know that he seems younger. He's had a bit of a rough start. My daughter has lost her way in life, and we almost lost Skylor because of it. I am very grateful that we didn't. He is my whole life now that my husband is gone. I don't know what I'd do without him. Hi, Quinn." this was directed to the tall, white-haired man I'd seen earlier today as he ambled over and clinked wine glasses with her.

She introduced us and explained a little of why I was there for a few weeks. (Somehow, "a few" sounded so much bet-ter than "five.") His smile was very friendly and warm as he welcomed me to their little group. He made no mention of the fact that he had seen me earlier, snooping around, and for this, I immediately liked him. I joked with him about his name on the town sign.

"That was just silly," he said, shaking his head. "Silly idea of a joke."

"It's quite true," Isabelle said earnestly. "It's an apt nickname. People look up to you, Quinn. You know they do."

She turned to me and continued, "I know that it's just a joke — the Mighty Quinn bit — but it's the truth that if anyone needs anything in this town, they all know who they can call. Quinn is our unofficial mayor."

"I thought that was Truman." Quinn grinned.

"Truman?" I asked.

"The dog."

"Oh, I've met him. He got in my car at the garage this morning."

"Oh sure. That would be Truman. He's just absolutely sure that everyone loves him as much as he loves everybody."

"Well, he's more lovable than the Little Brown Jug, I think."

"Oh, that fat bastard," this from Ale Murphy as he wandered into the conversation.

"He is that," Quinn agreed. I saw him exchange a grin with Isabelle, and I remembered that they had been good friends when their respective spouses had been living. I wondered if there was any romantic interest between them, not that it was any of my business. Nor any business of the L&G Detection Agency. Just human interest, I chuckled to myself.

I looked around in the frigid night air at the strange combination of people gathered together under the dark northern sky. It was bizarre, but I felt like I was part of the group. I smiled at the thought. Willie saw me and gestured to me to see if I wanted another glass of wine. I accepted one, and when I made my way over to her, I assured her that the next time I would buy and bring some wine.

That first night. I always look back on it with affection and warmth. It was probably because I had been so despondent earlier in the afternoon, and it turned out to be such a lot of fun. I guess that religious people would say that it was because I went to the church, but I think that it would have happened anyways—if not that night, then one soon thereafter—because in Truman Sound, everyone was linked with everyone else, and you couldn't stay there without being drawn into it.

That is why, when my brother called on Monday morning, I had just come in from a romp around with the dogs, and I was slightly breathless.

"Hey." His voice sounded pleased. "You sound all right up there. Have you forgiven me for sending you up to the back of beyond?"

"No, I have not. I think it would have been much easier for you, Lucas Cooper. Anyways, I was out taking Truman and Jugs for a walk."

"Jugs? Is Sally Big Boobs with you, Gill?"

10

I met the rest of the Singing Pines crowd simply by visiting
them. This was at Willie's suggestion. She explained that Mr.
Maindiaux and the Cathcarts were not very sociable, and if I was
going to interview them, I was just going to have to knock on
their doors. I did not relish the thought of doing this, as I really
had no protocol to follow, and I felt as if I were rushing in blind.
But I had a job to do, so I forged ahead.

Willie and Isabelle gave me some coaching first. I soon discovered that these two were quite good friends. Somehow, it
surprised me since they seemed to be of separate generations.
Willie, I guessed, was still in her thirties, whereas Isabelle was
past sixty. But they were great together, just great. They were
funny and full of ideas and life. I was very grateful to Willie for
the easy, friendly way in which she reached out her hand and

pulled me into the circle of her everyday round of days. This included many hours spent with Isabelle, and I was glad to be included in the warmth of their company.

Sometimes I felt guilty for enjoying it so much. I felt as if I should be detecting more and socializing less. But Willie and Isabelle reassured me that there were only so many people thereabouts to investigate and that I might as well be with them as sitting in my B&B room by myself.

When I look back, I don't know what I would have done if they hadn't befriended me. They turned my whole Truman Sound experience from black and white to amazing Technicolor. And I like to think that they enjoyed my company as well. They seemed to, anyways. I helped with crafts and quilting scraps while they told me little scenarios about the folks in the town so that I could get to know them that way, and I could feel as if I was working a little bit.

Isabelle's log cabin was the most quaint, cozy place that a person could imagine. There was a woodstove standing in the corner, dried herbs hanging from the rafters, and quilts draping across all the couches and love seats. These weren't displayed in a formal way, either. They seemed ready for snuggling under or lying on in front of the fire.

The main thing that I've always remembered about Isabelle Barnett's was the smell. She had cinnamon brooms hanging by the fire. They were simply naturally made brooms with the straw bristles scented with cinnamon sticks , and every so often a whiff of them would permeate the air in a delicious fashion. There was lavender about too, and Isabelle snipped this, along with the other herbs, for use in her cooking. I didn't know that you could actually use lavender in cooking.

I felt as if I could stay there with Willie and Isabelle for hours, listening to their chatting and laughter as they pursued their activities. They weren't idle—far from it. If Willie wasn't working on some craft or other for her Girl Guides, she was helping Isabelle with her quilting. And if all else failed, Isabelle had a basket of darning that she worked on as they talked their way through endless pots of tea. And that was another thing. They always drank Earl Grey tea. Ever since, I have associated it with friendship and good times.

Anyways, after they encouraged me and assured me that it would be fine to do so, I bit the bullet and decided to "interview" the other residents of Singing Pines. The first were the Cathcarts, and they were friendly enough in a very aloof manner. I had to chuckle to myself because they put me in mind of the people from back home, and as Sadie had told me, they were from my "neck of the woods." They certainly didn't offer anything like the warm arms of comradeship that had been extended to me by Willie and Isabelle.

I was invited in and asked if I would like a coffee, which I accepted as a way to prolong my visit. They were very polite and appeared to be full of care and concern, but all the time, I got the feeling that they could hardly wait for me to leave. Mr. Cathcart had been carving wood, and his wife had been reading the new Danielle Steele novel when I knocked on their door.

They made it very clear that they did not know Ryan Mainwright. Why on earth would they? They had come from the south to escape those tiresome teenagers who seemed to be everywhere. All they really wanted was some peace and quiet.

"Do you have any children of your own?" I asked, more by way of conversation than out of genuine interest.

"We do," she replied. "But they are in their thirties now and quite independent."

"No grandchildren?"

"No, thank God. Our kids are pursuing careers first. I have no desire to be a grandmother. I'm far too young. And I feel lucky to have survived raising my kids without any disasters."

For no reason at all, the thought of Isabelle Barnett and her obvious love for Skylor came unbidden into my mind. People were so different.

Mr. Cathcart was not quite so cut-and-dried. "Maybe someday we'll have some. And this will be a great place for them to come and visit. It's hard to tell in the winter, but the fishing and swimming in the summer are phenomenal."

"I can't imagine." I shuddered involuntarily. "It seems to me as if the whole town is frozen. Don't you miss the milder winters of Toronto?"

They both shrugged as if it really didn't matter.

"I actually like it here just fine," Mr. Cathcart said. "I do wood carvings, and I've got a heated garage, so I'm pretty well busy all the time. We were never really outdoors people anyways. Jean is happy with her books and satellite TV."

Jean Cathcart nodded her agreement. "I guess we're typical southerners. I don't get caught up in the social life here. I see that awful Murphy woman going back and forth to the Barnetts' with her brood and all the frivolity that goes on there. I can't bear it."

"Is she awful, do you think?"

"Why, certainly dear. Who would have so many children in this day and age? I'm telling you, it's obscene."

"Now, Jean."

"Well, that's just my opinion. I can't see it, myself. Typical small-town way of looking at things."

"What's that?"

"Why, having such a big family, of course. No one in Toronto would have so many children. They have much more class. I mean, you're supposed to reproduce only yourself, that's what I've always heard."

"What does that mean?"

"It means," she replied emphatically, "that two children should be your absolute limit."

"She seems like a good mother," Mr. Cathcart observed mildly.

Jean Cathcart sniffed. "All I can say is, some people just don't care about the population explosion."

"I guess some women are just more maternal than others," I said in an offhand manner.

She gave me a sideways glance as if unsure if she had been slighted or not, but I continued to look quite passive and noncommittal.

"Anyways," Mr. Cathcart continued, trying to keep hold of the conversational thread, "I can honestly say that I hardly knew Ryan Mainwright. He was a typical teenager—full of himself and preoccupied. It's an awful thing when a young person dies. It's a tragedy, because I'm sure that he would have turned into a decent young man."

"He wasn't a bad kid." This seemed like high praise coming from Jean Cathcart. "Ron's right. He was a typical kid. It's hard to know what personality they'll end up with after they've matured and discovered that they aren't the only people on the face of the earth. I think he was spoiled, really."

Ron Cathcart nodded his head fervently in agreement. "His dad wasn't too bad, but his mom thought that their family was better than the whole town of Truman Sound. That is not the attitude to adopt when coming to a little place like this. And it's pretty hard for the kid not to think he's something out of the ordinary when he hears his mother drilling it into his head that they are so superior."

"Do you think Ryan thought he was superior?"

The Cathcarts looked at each other uncertainly.

"It's really hard to tell," Ron said at last. "He was just a kid, really. Maybe he needed to be taken down a peg or two, as my old man used to say."

"Well, it wouldn't be by his old man," Jean said dryly. "He was too much under the thumb of the mother."

"He did seem a little henpecked."

"I think it was her who made an idiot of the boy. Made him think he was so good. Look where it got him."

"Do you think his attitude had anything to do with his murder?"

"Is it actually a murder? I thought the cops had laid it to rest."

"I don't know," I admitted. "I really don't know. All I know is that Barbara Mainwright thinks that the cops are missing something very important. I'm supposed to try to see if anything was missed. Not that I think I'm better than the cops," I hastened to add. "It's just that she came to our agency, and we agreed to see what we could find out."

"I think that you're going to be bitterly disappointed."

"I'm sure that you're right."

An uncomfortable silence ensued as I finished my coffee and hoped that another visit to this house was not going to be called for. Already, I was finding the natives of Truman Sound more to my liking than the natives of my own neighborhood—even after they'd been displaced for ten years.

"I'm not so sure it wasn't murder, though," Ron said thoughtfully into the pregnant pause.

His wife turned her head and looked at him in astonishment. "Why on earth would you say that?"

"Well, I always thought it was strange the way that boy was left there in the woods on his own. I don't ever remember seeing him without a whole pack of followers, male and female. And then, all of a sudden, he's found on a Monday morning, all by himself with a blow to his head. It's sad. You hear about that kind of thing in Toronto, but not up here. The people around here, they don't want to admit—or even think—that it might have been deliberate, but no one else came up with any plausible explanation, not that I ever heard of. I mean, it's pretty hard to get a blow to your head hard enough to kill you. He was young and healthy. He was a goddamned hockey player. I've thought about this a lot, and I just can't figure out how it could have happened."

Jean was looking at him as if he had just arrived from another planet. "I never heard any of this from you," she said in a skeptical tone, as if she were accusing him of being a sensationalist.

"You never asked," came the terse reply.

"I wish I could understand why anyone would want to hurt a boy of that age," I intervened in a bland tone. "It doesn't make any sense. Boys don't get killed for being conceited, or half the high school boys around would be eliminated."

Jean Cathcart sniffed. I could tell that as far as I was concerned, this interview was over. I sensed that she did not appreciate her husband divulging thoughts of any kind to me, especially those that he had not bothered to mention to his dearly beloved wife.

I hastily drained my coffee cup and murmured my thanks.

Ron was off on a mental tangent, though, and left me with a thought-provoking parting shot. "I just don't think that it's like in the movies and books," he said, "you know, where you examine the person's life and there's some long-buried motive. I mean, I bet that half of the murders that take place are just because of people being in the wrong place at the wrong time. There's no deep-seated motive at all. It's just the way the dice roll, and when it's your time, by George, it's your time."

This was far from a comforting thought for a poor little detective girl from Newmarket.

11

The next house on my list was the neglected-looking one that belonged to the Belgian man—the man I had high hopes for due to his sharing a nationality with "my friend Poirot," as Luke was so fond of calling him.

These hopes were very quickly dashed upon making the acquaintance of Claude Maindiaux. I knew that he was over eighty years of age, but the man who promptly responded to my timid rap on the door looked anything but old and feeble. He was tall and stern-looking. I remembered Sadie saying that he was a cross-country skier, and he certainly moved without any hesitation or stiffness. He peered at me over half-moon glasses as I explained the purpose of my visit.

"Humph. I've heard of you." His voice was gruff, and he spoke with what I thought was a French accent; when he asked me to come in, it was rather as if it was against his better judgment.

I tried to be friendly and professional. "I've never known anyone from Belgium, except for Hercule Poirot."

"Oh you knew him, did you?" He asked this with not even the slightest trace of a smile.

I swallowed abruptly and decided not to be intimidated. "I feel like I know him. I've been reading about him for ages and ages."

He looked me up and down as if to say that I hadn't, in his opinion, been alive for "ages and ages," and so really, I was not qualified to make such a decision.

I felt as if I had gotten off on the wrong foot completely when he asked me if I'd like a cup of tea, and I answered that since I was here, I might as well sit down.

"What have you heard about me then?" I looked at him directly and forced myself to smile as he set down two mugs with a teabag in each and a carton of skim milk on the bare wooden table.

"Oh, I might be old, but I do get out and hear things, you know. This town is like a cardboard box. There are only so many places you can go, and the talk is always the same. Probably because there's so damned little to talk about."

I sat still, waiting for him to go on.

He poured the boiling water over the tea bags and supplied me with a spoon to remove mine when it was the desired strength. Then he sat down across the table from me.

"You've come about that boy from the ritzy family, I've heard."

I nodded and sipped at my tea. I was trying to let him do the talking since I had to have something to write on the inevitable report. But it was like pulling teeth. His comments were slow and long-awaited. It was a good thing that I had a few weeks.

Finally, he leaned back in the chair and started to talk a little. "Ryan, wasn't it?"

Again I nodded.

"He sure thought he was the cat's meow, that kid. He wasn't unsure of himself at all, not like most kids his age. He'd swagger you know — not walk."

"Pretty conceited?"

"Is that what you call it?"

"I'm just asking. I didn't know him, of course. I know only what his mother told me. She thought he was wonderful."

"She was half of his problem. She made him think that he was better than everyone—at least, better than us simple folks around here. That's no good, you know. What did you say your name is?"

"Gillian."

"Humph. That's no good you know, Gillian."

I liked the way he said my name with his beautiful French accent, and I smiled at him.

"It's no good to think that you're better than others. It's no good to think that you're not as good as, either. We should all feel as if we are as good as the next fellow—not better, but as good as."

I nodded in agreement. "My parents certainly taught us that. But I think that Mrs. Mainwright thinks that she comes from a different social class than the people around here. Myself included," I hastened to add.

He snorted and humphed again. It seemed to be his favorite expression. "Socially, indeed. Silly cow of a woman. It must be a cold comfort to her now is all that I can say."

"Did you know Ryan at all?"

He shook his head. "I just saw him around town. I don't think that I ever saw him around Singing Pines. I told the police officer that. I would think that, in itself, was a little suspicious."

"What was?"

"Well, the fact that he was found here. I never once saw him on this road, and I usually see kids going back and forth all the time. All those Murphy kids and that little boy of Isabelle's. He's a broken little soul, if ever I saw one."

"Skylor?"

"Humph. Stupid name for a boy. Just asking for trouble."

"I think it's a nice name," I said, stung into retort. "And he is a very nice boy."

"He is indeed. Poor little bastard. He was a sorry sight when Reg and Quinn brought him home, I can tell you. Almost would have thought he was retarded or something. He's way better now. Almost normal. It was too bloody bad that Reg had to die so young. He and the boy were close."

"He seems okay, though."

Claude shrugged. "I guess so. But it's good for a boy to have a man in the house. I tell you, that's what's wrong with half of these kids today. They've got no fathers or else their fathers are deadbeats and can't be bothered with them."

"It's a good thing he's got Isabelle," I observed mildly.

"She's a good woman. That girl of hers was a lovely girl too. It was a crying shame when she got so involved with drugs. She went from a pretty little teenager to this ravaged-looking, dirty girl. Reg and Isabelle tried, but they just couldn't hold her. Heartbreaking is what I call it."

"That's awful."

"She's out west now, I hear. I used to know more when Reg was alive. He and I would have a coffee once in a while and chew the fat. I don't think they've heard from her in quite a few years now. All those junkies end up going out west."

"They do?"

"Why sure. It's warmer out there, and they can survive on the streets. You'd bloody freeze to death pretty quick around here if you were just lying around and doing drugs."

"It's cold, that's for sure."

"I just wonder sometimes what this world is coming to, you know." He shook his head in disparagement. "All these kids being raised by these parents who are so stoned half the time they don't know what's going on around them. That Skylor is lucky that he has family who cares about him. Lots of these kids don't. They just grow up to repeat the whole cycle that they're already caught in. Look at those two up the road." He thrust his head to the right. "Those two next to me up there."

"I haven't met them yet."

"Bloom is their name. Young couple. They've got this little boy, and how the hell do you think he will turn out?"

"I don't know them."

"Humph. They don't work. Neither one of them. Say they're looking but that there's no work up here. Humph. And that's their whole day—smoking weed. They have a little shed out back, and all day, one or the other is back there, puffing away."

"At least they're not in the house."

"Humph. You can smell it on them a mile away. Nice life for their kid. I don't care if you want to smoke your brains out, but why have a kid? How old do you think that kid is going to be before he twigs on to what's in the back shed? It's not that they're bad, really. They just do nothing. Nothing at all. And they're young. When I was their age, I was fighting for my country. And for what? I'm asking you. It's come to a sad way of life, I can tell you."

I felt as if we were miles away from our original topic, but I had no idea how to get back now. I decided to let myself go with the flow of Claude's conversation. After all, that is what Barbara Mainwright kept telling me—to talk to people on the street. And I didn't imagine that Claude had much opportunity to air his views, slanted though they may well be. My father had taught me to have respect for veterans. I reiterated this to Claude Maindiaux now.

"It was a wonderful thing that all the veterans did for us." I spoke humbly. "My father taught me always to respect having a free country and how lucky we are to live in Canada."

He softened visibly and actually broke into a little smile.

"Well, good for your father. A lot of kids were not taught that. They think it's a right to live in freedom, not a privilege. I still remember the invasion of Belgium by Nazi Germany in 1940. I was just under seventeen years old. These things—you never, never forget them. And the rows and rows of white crosses. All the young men who died."

"In Flanders Fields?"

"Yes. In Waregem Belgium, which is about fifty miles west of Brussels. There's over six acres of white crosses. All such young men."

He was silent for a moment, shaking his head in sorrow. And I remembered the words of my father: that the war never really left these men; that they carried it with them for the rest of their lives. His father had been in the war, and he had taught us this. I was glad now, as I watched this proud man, and I felt a stirring for him in my heart.

"My grandpa was in the war. That is why my father kept that faith alive in my brother and me."

"And you must pass it on as well, Gillian. I am glad to talk to you, mon cher. I did not want you to come," he said frankly. "You see, you never know. It is good for me. I tend to tar all young people with the same brush, but I can see that your father has taught you well."

I was absurdly pleased.

"There are a lot of good young people, Mr. Maindiaux."

"I suppose," he agreed grudgingly. "Just not around here."

"The Murphy kids seem like good kids."

"Humph. Give them time. They're young." But he smiled a little. "You're young enough that you still have faith in human nature, I guess," he said.

"Most of the time."

"I used to be a deacon at the Catholic Church. Not here. Further south. Anyways, one Sunday I was at mass—I was in the congregation that week—and I was sitting behind one of our very esteemed church members. She came to mass every week without fail and professed to be a good Christian. Anyways, when people went up for communion, I didn't go because I had strained my ankle and I preferred to kneel in the pew and pray. Are you familiar with the Catholic mass?"

I nodded.

"Then you will know how it goes. Everyone flocks to the front in two lines. As I said, I stayed in my seat, and this woman of whom I spoke—the pious one—she was kneeling as well, and I saw her slip her hand into a purse that was on the bench in front of her and pull out some money."

"That's awful. Do you know if she saw you?"

"I don't think so. But it put me off. I always figured that if you attended mass, you were at least trying to be a good person. It makes me sad, you know. There's not a lot of truly good people around, you know."

I didn't reply. I thought that he was a very cynical old man.

"That's why I like old Pete. He doesn't profess to be anything except what he is."

"Old Pete?"

"Yes, you know—he stays at Sadie's. Sadie and George are good to him."

"I know who you mean. He says 'bon jour' to me every morning. That's all I've ever heard him say."

"Or are likely to, is my guess. He walks around a bit, though. He's been here twice. Usually I go into Sadie's and have coffee with him. Sadie will often slip us a cookie or something."

I laughed. "She's good at that."

"Now there's a good person. And I don't suppose she's ever been inside a church in thirty years. She lives it."

I nodded. "That's what my mom always said about our dad. He didn't go to church with us much, but she always pointed out that he was a good person. My dad was always the first person to help someone out."

"It sounds like you come from good stock."

I figured that this was high praise coming from this crusty old Belgian, and I smiled my thanks as I got up and deposited my tea cup in his sink.

"I'm sorry I couldn't tell you more about the chap who was killed. I just don't know any more. And don't mind me going off on tangents. I'm old and don't have too many people to listen to me anymore."

I assured him that I had been happy to speak with him and that maybe I'd see him sometime if he was at Sadie's for a coffee.

"I'd like that," he said. "Oh, and Gillian ...," he called after me as I opened the door to the frozen air outside.

"Yes?"

"Now you know two Belgians."

"Pardon?" I had totally forgotten my earlier observation.

"Hercule Poirot and Claude Maindiaux."

And he closed the door with a parting chuckle.

12

I walked slowly out onto the snow-covered road and was trying to decide if I should go back to Sadie's or keep going. There were only the dope-smoking Blooms left on the street, besides Quinn and Isabelle. I could have summed this whole job up in five hours, I'm sure, instead of five weeks. I didn't know what more Barbara Mainwright expected of me. Just because she was paying didn't mean that there was much else up here that I could do. I couldn't just make stuff up so that she would have a satisfactory report.

As these thoughts were chasing each other about in my mind, a snowball went whizzing by my ear and landed in the bank beside me. I heard laughter and yelling behind me and turned to see Skylor Barnett and Fiona Murphy chasing each other around in circles, with Sean and Shay straggling along, trying to keep up.

"Gillian, Gillian, where are you going?"

For some reason, these kids had taken a shine to me, even though I had known them for only a few days. It was nice, actually. I'm sure it was because I was someone new and different, but they seemed to really enjoy my company, and they were always curious as to what I would be doing next. I hated to disappoint them. Although my life right now was far from exciting, it was gratifying to have their enthusiasm.

"I'm not really going anywhere. Just out for an afternoon stroll. Are you coming home from school?"

"Yes. Yes. Why don't you come to Nanabelles and have a cup of tea?"

"Well, I haven't really been invited," I started to explain, but they burst into laughter.

"You don't need an invitation to Nanabelles, silly."

"We just go there, you see," Fiona agreed. "My mom will be there too. Skylor and I will have a cup of milky tea and maybe a cookie or something to tide us over until suppertime. The little kids will have juice." She waved a hand to indicate her younger brothers.

As we all fell into step together and headed without further adieu toward the log cabin, the loud, shrill whistle of a train cut through the cold afternoon. I happened to catch a look on Skylor's face that seemed to be of utmost sadness. I saw Fiona put a friendly arm around his shoulders, and he smiled weakly at her. I had no idea how a train whistle could make someone feel so sad—even a child as sensitive as Skylor obviously was, but he soon recovered.

Turning to me, he asked, "Are you finding out about Ryan Mainwright's death? Nana said that you were a real live detective. That's just cool."

Ah, I thought, *maybe this explains their attraction to me. They think I am a detective, like on the TV shows that are so prevalent nowadays.*

"Well, I'm not really very experienced. My brother and I have a small business, and we try to help people if we can. Mrs. Mainwright came to us and asked us if we could find out what happened to Ryan. I mean, she knows that he died out in the bush across from Singing Pines, but she thought maybe I could find out a little more to …well, to make her feel a little better about it all," I finished feebly. I was not too used to kids this age, and I was unsure how much would be appropriate to tell them.

But Fiona nodded in a very worldly manner. "We know about it, Gillian. Don't worry. The police came and talked to all of us last year, but it happened late at night, and we didn't know anything about it until two days later."

"Did you guys know Ryan?"

"Ya," they spoke in unison and looked at each other.

I was curious. They seemed a little unsettled by the question. "What's up?" I asked, keeping my voice casual.

"Nothing." Again, in unison.

We all laughed then.

"You guys are a big help," I observed ruefully. "I asked only if you knew him. Maybe I should have asked if you liked him."

"He was good-looking," Fiona said. "And he had lots of girl friends. But he thought he was pretty cool. Do you know what I mean, Gillian? Did they have boys like that when you went to school?"

"Sure."

I sighed inwardly. I must be getting past my bloom of youth if this girl thought it was quite a while since I was in school.

"I didn't like him very much," Skylor volunteered.

"You didn't?"

I wondered if Skylor had been a little jealous of Ryan. It's hard to associate with someone like that at the best of times, let alone when you've had a bit of a rough start yourself.

"He was mean to Skylor. I didn't like him either," Fiona said with loyal conviction.

I wondered if she felt bad for commenting on Ryan's good looks earlier. She seemed to be pretty tight friends with Skylor Barnett.

"Mean to you? Was he, Skylor?"

Skylor shrugged. "He wasn't really mean to me. He just wasn't nice, is all."

"Once he took his backpack and wouldn't give it back, and Skylor didn't have any lunch."

Skylor shrugged again. "It was really no big deal."

"Well, it certainly wasn't very nice," I observed. "He sounds like a bit of a bully."

"Oh, he was," Fiona agreed. "Only he always turned things around and charmed the teachers, and he never got into any real trouble. He always came out smelling like a rose—even the day he took Skylor's backpack. Aunt Izzy went to the school to complain, but Ryan just turned the whole thing around to make it look like a game and as if Skylor was complaining about nothing."

"I don't think that he sounds like a very nice boy." I was thinking that I was getting a lot more information out of these teenagers than I had out of all of the adults on the street. The adults hadn't really known him, I guessed. These kids had known him firsthand.

"Well, he was all right sometimes," Fiona admitted grudgingly. "Once my bike got a flat tire, and he gave me a lift in his truck. He was nice that day."

"Was he quite a bit older than you?"

Fiona nodded.

"I'm almost fourteen, and Sklyor's fifteen, and he was two years ahead of Skylor. I guess he just couldn't be bothered with kids that much younger than him."

We were approaching the log cabin now, and I could see that Fiona was right about her mother being here. I could see her snowshoes and poles stuck in the snowbank beside the inukshuk. Today the inukshuk was sporting a toque, but instead of a tassel at the end, it had a net contraption filled with suet and birdseed.

"Who changes his hat?" I inquired.

"Whose? Chuck's?"

"Is that his name? Apropos, I guess."

"It suits him, if that's what you mean. And we all change his hat. Whoever wants to. There's no rules—as long as he's got something on. The birds have to be able to eat something."

"I'd say the birds around here do pretty well."

"It's so cold up here, you see," Skylor came close to me and spoke in his shy, quiet way. "There's not a lot for them to eat. So Nanabelle and I feed them every day. They've become very tame. They trust us."

"Skylor has a couple of chickadees that will eat the seed right out of his hand."

What a strange, gentle sort of boy he was. He opened the door to the log cabin politely for the smaller boys, Fiona, and me. He wasn't like any fifteen-year-old boy that I'd ever known. I smiled my thanks at him.

The thought came unbidden into my head that he was in sharp contrast to the boy who was the subject of my inquiries. You'd have to be a real bully to take a lunch from this child. He was so fragile. It would be the height of cruelty.

Maybe Ryan Mainwright hadn't been the lovely boy his mother was proclaiming he was. Maybe she was protesting too loudly.

13

"Nana!" Skylor called out as he closed the door behind us. "Are you here?"

Isabelle and Willie were sitting at the kitchen table with cups of tea in front of them. A big blue teapot was between them. I could smell the delicious aroma of freshly baked cookies intermingled with the lavender and cinnamon scents that always hung around the corners of Isabelle's cabin. Skylor and the Murphys were not to be disappointed in the anticipation of baked goods today.

I had the impression that this was generally a pretty great place to come after school. Again, I got a feeling of going back in time. Most kids this age whom I knew had to be quite responsible and stay alone for a few hours after school. Not this bunch! They had it made. I'd have liked to come home here myself.

I smiled at them, still a little unsure of myself. "The kids told me to come with them. I met them up the road."

"Well, of course, Gillian. I'm glad to see you. Pull up a chair."

As she spoke, Isabelle was bustling about setting out another mug for me and getting a plate of cookies for the youngsters. She was pouring juice for the younger boys and milky tea for Fiona and Skylor, just as Fiona had predicted.

Willie, meanwhile, was pulling up her chair close to me and asking, with undisguised enthusiasm, "How's the sleuthing going? Have you found out anything earth-shattering yet? Or aren't you allowed to say?"

I laughed and accepted the tea and a chocolate chip cookie. I was going to have so much caffeine on board that I might not sleep for a few days. Still, I didn't want to be left out of this cozy little gathering by refusing a cup of tea.

"Honestly, Willie, there's nothing to tell. I don't know how on earth Mrs. Mainwright expects me to actually work for five weeks. There are only five houses on this street, and I've talked to everyone around here now. If nobody knows anything, I can't just make it up."

"Of course you can't. She's a very silly woman who can't accept her son's death. Not," Willie hastened to add, "that I think it would be easy. I think that it's every parent's nightmare, and I don't wish it on my worst enemy. But she struck me as a person who always had to blame someone else for everything. I mean, maybe it was a complete and utter accident. It's tragic, but maybe there really is no mystery."

"I don't really think it's a mystery either," I admitted. "But they're insisting that I stay here and look around. I have no idea what I'll do for four more weeks."

"Oh, I do." Isabelle sat down, after making sure that everyone had some form of refreshment, and smiled warmly at me. "Why don't you just enjoy yourself? Winter is so much fun up here."

"Sometimes at home we have hardly any snow at all. If it wasn't so cold, you'd never know that it was winter."

"That's what I mean. I figure if it's going to be cold, you may as well get snow, and then you can enjoy it to some degree. There's so much more to do."

"For sure," Willie agreed. "Take Isabelle and me. Every morning after the bus comes, we exercise for one hour, no matter what. In the nice weather, we walk, but now that we've got snow, we snowshoe."

"I'm impressed."

"Some days we impress ourselves."

I laughed.

"No, really." Willie went on earnestly. "About three years ago, Isabelle and I decided that we wanted to try to get a little fitter. We didn't particularly want to lose weight."

This alone made them different from any females I had ever encountered in my entire life.

"There are no gyms around, unless you want to drive for an hour or so. We didn't want to do that, so we just made up our minds that we would make ourselves exercise for a minimum of an hour every morning. It's good to be partners too, because if one of us is dragging her ass, the other one tries harder."

"And vice versa," Isabelle laughed. "You'd be more than welcome to come, Gillian. It's not because we are exclusive that it's stayed only the two of us."

"It's just that there's no one else about."

"I don't have any snowshoes."

"I may be able to scare up an extra pair," Isabelle offered. "Mary, who sings in the choir with me . . ."

"They are the choir. The two of them. The whole choir."

"Okay, smarty. Mary, who *is* the choir with me, has a pair that her daughter used to use, but she moved away. I bet she'd let you use them."

"That would be great." The prospect of getting out and doing something sounded good. Truman Sound was proving to be much friendlier than I had originally anticipated, but the remaining time that stretched out in front of me still seemed endless. Any diversion was welcome. "Not that I've ever snowshoed."

They both waved my concerns away, assuring me that there was nothing to it, nothing at all. They'd be glad to have company. I would be their inspiration.

"We can show you around the woods where Ryan died," Willie told me in an undertone. "You can incorporate it into your investigation so you'll feel as if you're getting something done work-wise at the same time"

"Did you get a chance to talk to any of the folks on the street yet, Gillian?" Isabelle asked. "I hope they were friendly. Some of them tend to keep to themselves."

"Not like Izzy and me." Willie winked, and they both laughed.

"I met the Cathcarts and Claude Maindiaux. And I think you're right. I think that they both could have done without my visit."

"It's not you," Willie assured me. "I think they got fed up to their teeth with the Mainwrights when they were here."

"They don't seem to have been very well-liked."

Isabelle and Willie looked at each other as if considering this.

"It's not really that," Isabelle said. "It's more that she felt we were all way beneath them—Mrs. Mainwright, in particular."

"That's about what I've heard."

"This is a very small town, and everyone is friendly, you know. You'll find a lot of little northern places are like that. People are always welcome to join us at any time. But the Mainwrights didn't want to mingle at all."

"She sure wouldn't have wanted to come snowshoeing with us," Willie agreed. "And we wouldn't have asked her. She was just that type of person. I'm sure you know people like that. It's just more pronounced when there aren't many people around. Anyways, was Claude all right with you? He can be a crusty old bugger."

"Actually, he wasn't too bad. I don't think that he liked me at first. I made the mistake of saying that the only other Belgian I knew was Hercule Poirot."

"How was that a mistake? Doesn't he like Agatha Christie?"

"I don't know. He didn't say. He just said, 'Oh, you knew him did you?' I felt like a fool."

"Well, if you read enough books about a certain person, they do become almost real to you."

"Thank you, Isabelle." I felt ridiculously pleased by her understanding what I'd meant.

"I've always preferred Miss Marple myself. I liked the way she sat in the corner and knit and put all those pompous policemen to shame."

"My mom always liked her. We used to watch the old episodes, when Joan Hickson was Jane Marple. She wasn't as showy as my Poirot."

"Not by a long shot. She always compared her range of suspects with people whom she knew from her little village, alleging that human nature was basically the same everywhere." Isabelle explained this to Willie, who looked as if she was trying and failing to understand the thread of our conversation.

I turned that around in my mind. I tended to forget about Miss Marple. Maybe later I would try to see if I could compare the residents of Singing Pines to my network of acquaintances back home. I was going to have to write down some account of my time.

"My God," Willie laughed. "I thought that it was just Isabelle and me who got sidetracked in our talking. But I see it can happen to anyone."

"Of course it can. It would be too boring otherwise. Did Claude warm up to you, Gilly?"

I glanced up in surprise, and she grinned.

"Sorry, that slipped out. My sister had a friend named Gillian, and we never called her anything except Gilly."

"That's okay."

"You don't mind?"

"Oh my, no. My mom always called me Gilly."

At this moment, Skylor and Fiona swept through the kitchen with their eyes on the plate of cookies, and they both started to laugh.

"Willie and Gilly. Gilly and Willie."

"How old are you two?" Isabelle inquired, but she too was grinning.

I laughed as well. "Anyways, Claude warmed up to me when I talked to him a little, and I ended up quite liking him. I told him my grandpa was in the war and I knew a little about it, which helped."

"A lot of veterans are a little off when they get older. They've seen so much. My grandfather," Willie said, "was in the war too, and once in a while, he would go off like a loony toon."

"Mine, too. Not," I added hastily, "that he was a loony, but certain things would set him off, and my dad would nod to us to just let him be. And he always came around, eventually."

"Claude is actually a very good man," Isabelle declared. She came across as a person who would always try to see the goodness in someone. This reminded me of my mom again. Sometimes it was annoying, but when you were the one who required mercy, it was not a bad thing, not a bad thing at all.

"Oh, he's all right," conceded Willie. "He's just not warm and fuzzy, that's all."

"How many people actually are?"

At this very moment, Skylor and Fiona again descended on the room and answered this question as naturally as if it had been intended for them.

"Well, we are."

"You are what?"

"Warm and fuzzy."

"We are?"

"Well sure."

"Which of us?"

"All of us. You know, you and me and Mom and Quinn and Gillian."

"Me, as well?" I had to interject. I was incredibly flattered to be included in this little survey.

"Sure. Skylor and I know these things. We have a sixth sense."

"I see."

"Did you want to come upstairs and see some of Skylor's paintings?"

"Is it all right?" I directed the question to the adults.

"Oh, of course," Isabelle assured me. "It's not everyone who gets invited up there, Gillian. You should feel flattered. It must be because of your warmth and fuzziness."

I sensed an inward chuckle behind her words.

"I am flattered," I said, rising to the occasion, literally and figuratively. "I'd love to see Skylor's paintings."

Skylor himself was looking quite bashful, but he allowed me to be led up the stairs behind him, and Fiona chatted all the way, as was her wont.

I thought that Fiona was the epitome of a loyal friend. And for some reason, which I felt rather than thought, I knew instinctively that Skylor could use such a person.

14

I had never been inside a log cabin before, and its upstairs was like nothing I had ever seen. It was beautiful, so natural and wonderfully crafted. Reg Barnett must have been a great man to have produced such a lasting tribute to his talent. Everything about that house was warm and cozy and friendly. I felt as if I had been there a thousand times before, in a thousand other lives. I never got over the feeling in Truman Sound that I had stepped back in time.

There were three bedrooms at the far end of the hall, but the room that commanded the most attention was the huge room above the downstairs living room. It was set up as a workshop, with different equipment in various areas.

Skylor and Fiona were twirling around, showing me this and that, and the two younger boys were peeking out of the corners. I felt inspired by their youthful exuberance. I was only twenty-seven, but I felt quite removed from this utter enthusiasm and energy.

Isabelle had a quilting frame set up on one side of the big room, and there was a quilt with all the colors of the rainbow stretched out on it. Beside it stood an old-fashioned table with a sewing machine and so many piles of scraps and threads and pattern pieces that there was virtually not one square inch to spare. It reminded me of the type of jumble that used to adorn our spare table at home before Mom acquired the shop. It looked like a mess, but if anyone moved a single thing, my mom would know it.

Skylor and Fiona said as much of Isabelle's table.

"It looks like a great big pile of stuff, but Aunt Izzy knows where everything is. If you touch anything at all, she can tell."

"I wouldn't dream of touching a thing," I said hastily. "My mom used to do crafts. I know the rules."

"There is order in her disorder."

"He's quoting Aunt Izzy now," Fiona explained.

"Oh, I see. It seems to fit."

They both nodded, and I was guessing that this was one of the basic rules. They could be up here as long as they touched nothing.

There was another, smaller table set up behind the quilting table, and it seemed to be a scrapbooking centre. There were pages and photos and little quotes in abundance—again, in ordered disorder, I was guessing.

"This is the only craft that I ever really caught on to," I said. "My mom used to run a craft store back home. Before she bought it, our spare room looked just like this."

"Did she sell it?"

"No, not really. My brother Lucas and I are using it for our detection agency."

"Cool!" they exclaimed together, almost on the same breath.

"Oh, it's not really. We don't get any big fancy cases like on TV. We just do a bit of security work and help people. There are lots of people who want odd jobs done who just can't do them themselves or who don't have time. We do whatever we have to do to make a living. People get to know that at least we're reliable."

"I still think it sounds cool," Skylor declared. "That's why you got sent on this big case, right, Gilly? Because people count on you."

I went over and ruffled his hair. "I don't want you to think of me as someone like that, Skylor. I'm just an ordinary girl. My brother took law and security, and I trained as a PSW. Do you know what that means?"

They both shook their heads.

"It's called a personal support worker. It means that you go around and do jobs for people who can't do them for themselves. I used to work in a nursing home, but I didn't really like it. I have much more freedom with this job."

"Quinn's wife was in a nursing home before she died. It was awful."

"They are not very cheerful places," I agreed. "But they are very necessary."

"Well, I hope I die before I have to go to one," Fiona said merrily. "I remember how sad Quinn used to look when he came home from visiting Rose. I was just little, but I remember because he was usually so great. I heard Mom say that his wife got garbage pneumonia at the end."

"I never heard of that."

"I know what it is," Skylor spoke up. "It's when you lie around in bed all the time, and it happens after a while, and when you get pneumonia, you can't eat at all because everything you do eat ends up in your lungs."

"Sounds terrible." I was not sure how accurate this information was.

"It was awful for Quinn. He's such a nice guy."

"Quinn's great," Skylor agreed.

"Glad you think so too." Fiona looked at her friend slyly. "He seems to like you guys too."

"What guys?"

"You guys in this house."

"Nana and me? Of course he likes us. He's always been our friend. He was Papa's best friend."

"Maybe he likes Aunt Izzy a little more than 'just friends.'"

Skylor blushed, from his chin on up to the tip of his nose. "I don't think so," he mumbled.

I was looking on with curiosity. I remembered listening to the grownups when I was a kid, trying to glean information. These two seemed to be in the know about lots of things—or else they were just manufacturing facts. Either way, it was interesting. I thought again that perhaps I would get further ahead by speaking with the kids, who had not yet learned to censor their verbal output, than with the adults who had.

"I'm just saying," Fiona went on loftily, "that they think a lot of each other."

"Of course they do."

"Like the night before Aunt Izzy had her foot operation, and Quinn stayed here with her. You were at our place, remember?"

"Of course I remember. Nana explained all that to me. He was driving her to the hospital in the morning, and they had to leave early. And she was worrying because of that thing that she has wrong with her heart."

"I forgot about that thing." Fiona looked a little abashed and hastened to explain. "I wasn't saying anything bad about her, Skylor. You know I'd never do that. I just always wondered about them. They seem to be pretty close. Your Nan is still a real nice-looking lady, you know."

"I do know that."

"What has she got wrong with her heart?" I ventured to ask.

"I forget the name. It's a bunch of initials. It's the reason Nanabelle always worries when I get a sore throat."

"A sore throat?" Again, the conversation was leaving me behind.

Fiona elaborated, "It's some kind of bug that you get from strep throat, and it can go down to your heart."

I felt skeptical, but said nothing. Certainly, I had never heard of this.

"Nana says that it doesn't happen so much anymore because there are more antibiotics now. But she says there are some people who are her age who had it. Anyways, that's why Quinn came and stayed overnight. And Nana told me that having a good friend who you can count on to help you like that is the best thing in the world. I know she would have told me if it were anything else. I'm old enough to know."

"Of course you are," I said reassuringly.

"I bet you're right, Sky," I got the feeling that Fiona was sorry for teasing her friend, even in her gentle way. "I mean, look at us. We're the very best of friends aren't we? And we're not girlfriend and boyfriend. We're just happy hanging around together."

Skylor sent her a smile as warm as the sun.

"Of course we are," he agreed.

And I thought that these two were very lucky indeed.

15

After all of these issues were straightened out to everyone's satisfaction, we turned to look at the remainder of the big craft room. And that was when I got the shock of my life.

The whole back half of the room was devoted to an easel and opened tubes of paint and lots of canvasses in varying stages of completeness. This room, too, was in a form of disarray, but the completed projects were simply breathtaking. Even though I had heard rumblings that Skylor Barnett was very talented, I had no idea of the magnitude of that talent. I was by no means an art critic, but I knew how very exceptional these pieces were.

"My God, Skylor," I breathed. "These are incredible—absolutely incredible."

"Aren't they?" Fiona was on firm ground here. She, too,

knew a good thing when she saw it, even though I got the feeling that she would be on Skylor's side in most things.

Skylor blushed again. I didn't know that teenage boys could blush like that. I thought it was pretty cute, but I pretended not to notice.

Amazed, I started to look at some of the completed works. They were very easily recognizable, but it wasn't just that. It was the depth and color of what was portrayed. There was one picture of what I took to be a Saturday night on the Truman River, with all the kids skating and the lights strung up on the trees. Although you could tell that the scene took place after dark, you could still discern the various people, and even a few of Skylor's beloved birds hovered about. Oh, and there was Mr. Chuck with a big straw hat on and several birds pecking at his brim. In the distance were traces of the northern lights.

"This is fantastic. I've don't think that I've ever seen a picture more lifelike than this. This is Truman Sound on a Saturday night, isn't it?"

Skylor nodded.

"I love that one too," Fiona agreed. "Everybody looks so real-as if they were going to start moving any time. And can you see them dancing, Gillian?"

I looked closer and knew I could look for a long time and not see everything in the painting. There was so much detail, and so many different little things were happening. It must have taken Skylor forever to have painted this.

"Oh, yes. I didn't realize that was what they are doing, but now I see. Don't forget, I've been here for only one Saturday night."

"We'll fix that in about two days," Skylor grinned. He seemed quite relaxed now. I imagined that this was his place in the world where he was the most at ease.

"We will indeed."

"It will be good because Haven McPhee will be here with his fiddle, and then everybody gets to dance—if they want to. It's so much fun to watch. He comes the weeks we don't have mass.

They're my favorite Saturdays. No mass and a longer party and fiddle music. Sometimes my dad brings his guitar, and then we have a lot of music. It's a blast!"

It did seem very curious indeed—Ale Murphy and Haven McPhee playing music together on the banks of a river. A person just could not make this stuff up even if he wanted to.

"Anyways, you can see Haven with his fiddle, and these people here," Fiona indicated a plethora of colorful figures that seemed to be in motion, "are dancing to 'Truman Sound Saturday Night.'"

I was totally confused now. I thought these kids had lost their faculties.

"Haven't you heard of it, Gilly? It's a song."

"Are you guys pulling my leg?"

"No. Skylor's right. It is a song, but the real title is 'Sudbury Saturday Night.' Do you know it?"

"I don't think so."

"It's sung by Stompin' Tom Connors."

"Oh, yes." Somewhere came a distant note of recollection from my past. "I think that my Uncle Murray used to like him, and we were forced to listen to some of his music."

"You didn't like him?"

"I'm just not a real country and western fan."

"My papa used to like him. He said he was a real Canadian. I like some of his songs. They're funny—like 'Bud the Spud.'"

"You're right. I don't remember this Sudbury one, though."

That was all that was needed. It was as if I'd flipped a switch. Fiona grabbed Skylor's arm and started swinging him around in the middle of the big room, while the smaller boys mimed the playing a guitar and a fiddle.

They all sang:

Oh the girls are out to bingo
And the boys are getting stinko
And we'll think no more of Inco
On a Truman Sound Saturday Night.

"What is going on up here?"

I turned to see Willie and Isabelle ascending the stairs amid the breathless laughter that filled the room.

"We were just singing the Saturday night song to Gillian. She hasn't heard it."

I laughed and clapped my hands. "That was quite a performance. I can hardly wait to see the real thing."

"Stick around," Willie chuckled. "It's not that great."

"When you live in a place so isolated and with so few folks, you have to make your own fun, or you wouldn't have any at all. It's kind of fun to dance outside, by the river. It keeps us going. As cold as it is, we always end up sweating."

"I can see why you guys don't need a gym." I observed. "I'm hoping that my brother Luke will be able to come up one weekend before I go home. He's going to try."

"That will be nice for you, dear."

"He's the other great detective," Fiona declared, and she and Skylor giggled together.

"I told you, that's not true. We're really ordinary—not very exciting."

"To us, you're not ordinary," Skylor grinned.

"Well, you're not very ordinary yourself, young man." I turned to Isabelle. "These paintings are incredible. This grandson of yours has an amazing talent."

Isabelle nodded. "He is very good. I tell him that every day."

"She does," Fiona agreed. "And I do too."

Skylor was not blushing this time, but he looked very bashful indeed and simply said, "Thank you."

"I can't believe it, Isabelle. This picture of the river on a Saturday night—which is what started the whole demonstration of the song—is one of the most beautiful, detailed pictures I've ever seen. I feel like I'm standing right there." My gazed turned to Sklylor, and I asked, "What grade are you in?"

"I'm only in grade nine. I should be in grade ten, but I'm not."

"And I'm glad," Fiona chirped in, "because we're in the same grade. He's my best friend, not my boyfriend."

"Which is much better," Isabelle agreed, which brought to mind the comments regarding her status with Quinn.

"I was asking only because we have such a great art college in Toronto. It's neat. It's built up on stilts, and it's got all kinds of funky art exhibits and neat three D art and big pictures. I've seen some of them and they are not one half—no, not one quarter—as good as these paintings. These are amazing."

"Is that near where you live?" Skylor asked.

"Well, it is compared to from here. It's all relative, I guess. It would be an hour or so from our place. It's not really all that far, but it's the traffic that takes up so much time."

"I can't even imagine that much traffic."

"It is hard to imagine up here. But it's a really good college," I turned to Isabelle. "He is so talented."

Isabelle nodded slowly. "I know he is. It will be quite a while from now, though, before we have to think about things like college."

I heard Skylor give a sigh. Was it of relief? I hadn't thought of it before, but now I wondered how a boy like this would ever survive in the outside world. I thought about his grandmother; she must worry about this very thing. It was hard to imagine Skylor existing anywhere except right here. He seemed so fragile—almost childlike—although in some ways, he was quite mature. I never could quite put my finger on this quality that was present in Skylor, and I thought about it a lot. I wondered if those first few years had taken their toll on him, even if he had no recollection of them. And who knew what effect the drugs that he had inadvertently received by way of his mother had on him. Maybe someday Isabelle would tell me the whole story. It was hard to believe that such a caring woman could have a daughter who was so neglectful of her own child.

Fiona was on a roll, over by the canvasses, to prove that she was Skylor's biggest fan.

She had pulled a few of them out for my benefit, and I was duly impressed. I could hardly fathom that these magnificent works of art had been produced by this shy slip of a boy who stood at my side.

The last one that Fiona reached for was apparently his latest masterpiece. It was a face, and it was in black and white, with the only color being a red toque perched high on the subject's head. The face was an amazing blend of lines and outlines, with crinkles around eyes that sparkled with an inner light. As I looked closer, I saw that there was the faintest hint of blue inside the irises. I realized that I recognized that handsome, craggy face.

"Why, it's Quinn!" I exclaimed.

"So it is," said Willie. "Skylor, that is incredible. You are getting to be one hell of an artist."

"I painted it for Quinn for Christmas," Skylor explained. He turned to me and said, "Quinn is always helping Nan and me, and I wanted to do something for him. It's the first face I've ever done, not counting just fooling around."

"Wow! Skylor, I am truly amazed."

"Do you think he'll like it?"

"He'll love it."

Isabelle nodded her agreement, and Skylor looked very pleased.

I looked around the room, trying to take in the degree of talent that was manifest here.

"I just can't believe how talented you guys are. This room is loaded with genius, I think."

We heard a male voice calling a greeting from the downstairs.

"It's Quinn," Skylor gasped in dismay. "Quick, hide that picture so he doesn't see it."

"We'll go down," Isabelle said. "He'll be ready for a cup of tea. He went to Timmins today and picked up some material for me at the fabric store there."

"He picked some stuff up for me too," said Willie, as we traipsed down the stairs to the sweet-smelling kitchen. "We don't have a Walmart or anything like that here, Gillian. So if there's anything you need, you might ask Quinn to pick it up for you. He goes to Timmins about every week or so. Sometimes in the winter, it's really hard to get out."

My God, I thought, *not only do I feel like I'm in another world, but I also feel like I'm on a whole other planet.*

16

The next day, I joined Willie and Isabelle for snowshoeing. I had been hesitant in the morning — not really shy, but a little uncertain. I was drinking a cup of Sadie's excellent coffee and debating with myself about heading down to Singing Pines when George came out and told me that there was a phone call for me.

He grinned as he held out the phone. "Making friends already, I see."

Sadie smiled approvingly.

It was Willie, and she told me that Isabelle had obtained the snowshoes from Mary and that I was welcome to use them for as long as I wanted to.

"So you just head on over here, my dear. Isabelle and I will wait 'til you get here."

"Is that okay? I don't want to hold you up."

Willie assured me that they were not in a hurry today and that they were looking forward to my company. I bundled up and braved the frigid morning air. I headed down the road, which was now becoming quite familiar to me.

Isabelle and Willie were waiting at the log cabin, as promised. I took a minute to stop and admire Chuck, who had changed his attire again and was now wearing a red scarf and toque with birdseed strung all along each item. *That inukshuk has a bigger wardrobe than I do*, I thought ruefully.

The birds certainly approved of the outfit Skylor selected. There was such a flock of blue jays, cardinals, chickadees, and finches that they seemed to be having a party of their own.

"Skylor never forgets to feed them," Isabelle gestured at them as she saw me gazing at them in wonder. "Those birds are better fed than a lot of families."

"And I was just thinking that the inukshuk has more accessories that I do."

We all were laughing as Isabelle produced the snowshoes from inside the shed.

"I hope they fit. My feet are pretty big."

"They don't go by the size of your feet," Willie explained. "They go by your weight. There are only two sizes, one is for less than 150 pounds, and the other, for over 150. We are glad that you can fit into Mary's daughters because Isabelle and I both need the bigger-sized ones."

They giggled together, like a couple of school girls.

"You see, Gilly dear, you're young," Isabelle started to explain, "and you're cute and little, but after you have a couple of kids …"

"Or five."

"Well, your weight climbs a little, and even though you try to be active, there's only so much you can do."

I would not have thought that either of these ladies would have been over the cutoff weight, and I said so.

"You're a dear, really, but we hover around there, you know."

"Hover?"

"Well, some days a little more, some a little less, depending on which way the wind blows."

"Or what we ate for dinner last night."

We were all laughing now. It was hard not to like these ladies, with their easy laughter and their careless disregard of their weights. I did not know one woman, of any age, amongst my acquaintances, who would be so flippant about and comfortable with the numbers on her scale. It was quite refreshing, actually.

"Also, we don't want to have to worry if we want to bring a backpack. We don't want a water bottle or a snack to tip us over the limit enough so that we sink into the snow."

"Brilliant," I observed, still laughing.

I got my snowshoes strapped on with very little trouble and proceeded to follow them across the road and through the woods on what I supposed was a snowmobile trail. I was amazed at the density of the bush and how utterly isolated it really was. I was extremely glad to be in the company of these two, who knew the woods so well. I would never have ventured off the road on my own.

"Nervous?" Isabelle glided up beside me and smiled.

"Not really. I'm just not used to being so far away from houses and people. I guess I'm just a city girl."

"That's okay. There's nothing to hurt you in these woods, you know. In the summer, there are bear, and there are often deer and moose, but they are more afraid of you than you are of them."

"Are you sure?"

"Yes, dear, I'm sure. I've lived in these parts almost my whole life now. I know these woods like the back of my hand. Nothing will hurt you here."

In direct contradiction to Isabelle's words, Willie, who was a little ahead of us, turned around and pointed at a little clearing in the pine trees.

"That is where the Mainwright boy died," she said.

I shuddered involuntarily and looked. I don't know what I was expecting to see, but of course, there was nothing at all to indicate that any trauma had ever taken place there. Anything that may have once been there was covered with a foot of snow. I said as much out loud.

"That was the same problem as on the day after it happened," Willie noted. "There was so much snow that Ryan himself was almost covered."

"At one time, I would have thought that was very early for snow, but I've learned differently now. When I stopped in Haileybury on the drive up, the little apple doll lady I met told me the history of the big fire in 1922, and she said that the next day it snowed—and that was October fifth, for heaven's sake. I never would have dreamed that snow could come so early. It must make the winters very long."

"Oh, it does. That's why we have to get out and do things. If we just sat in the house and did nothing, it would be even longer."

"I suppose. Well, at least I can tell Barbara Mainwright that I've been investigating. I have to call her tonight. I have no idea what to tell her, but I can't put it off any longer."

We snowshoed for a little longer before I asked, "Who found Ryan, anyways? I don't think I ever learned that."

Willie and Isabelle looked at each other.

"A friend of his, I think," Willie said. "They were supposed to go snowmobiling—or something—and Ryan wasn't home. I guess he often stayed out quite late, and his parents thought that he was in bed after the night before. When his friend came down from North Bay to meet him, they just thought that he was being idle. Then they discovered that he wasn't in his bed and had never come home at all. They called the police, and everyone started looking. Truman Sound is so small that it didn't take long to find him. Although what he was doing over at Singing Pines, I never did find out. Do you know, Izzy?"

Isabelle shook her head. "I never heard too much, really, because that was the day I had surgery on my foot. I stayed at the hospital in Timmins overnight, and I missed all the excitement. Don't you remember, Will? You had Skylor for me. Not that that is noteworthy," she laughed, "because he spends half of his time at your place without a valid reason."

"What happened to your foot?" I asked.

This was the night that I'd heard Skylor and Fiona talking about, and I was dying to hear the whole story, but I didn't want to seem too nosy. I wondered if Quinn's name would come up.

"Oh, I had bunion surgery. I had to have a cast on my foot for the following six weeks, and I missed everything that was going on."

Nothing more to be found out on that front today it seemed, not that it had anything at all to do with why I was here. Being of the female sex, though, I was always ripe for a little gossip.

I pulled myself back to the task at hand and thought aloud about what I would tell Barbara Mainwright.

"Well, you can tell her that you've interviewed a lot of people and you're talking to people all the time to find out if they remember anything. Who do you have left, anyways?"

"Just the Blooms and Quinn on Singing Pines."

"That won't take long."

"Let's turn around now. This is pretty good for your first day. And we are obliged to do only one hour. Let's have a cup of coffee, with just a little touch of Baileys, to take the chill out of our bones. And you can figure out what to say to her so you sound professional."

We all laughed as we headed back to the blessed warmth of the log cabin, with its beautiful fireplace and sweet smell of cinnamon and lavender.

That night, I called the Mainwrights' number, as I promised myself I would. A part of me was longing to get an answering machine, or at least Mr. Mainwright, but that was not to be. It was Barbara Mainwright's high-pitched, slightly whiney voice that answered on the second ring.

I explained to her what I had done so far and that I had visited the scene of the crime (for what it was worth) and that I had found out the absolute square root of zero. She didn't care. She wanted me to stay the allotted time and keep "sleuthing."

"Mrs. Mainwright, I feel guilty. You're paying me a lot of money, and I'm not so sure that there's anything more to find out."

"Never mind the money. It means nothing to me," she said harshly. "You keep looking, Miss Cooper. And I don't care how nice you think those small-town, little people are. One of them killed my son."

17

It was the next day that I experienced the full glory of a Saturday night in Truman Sound, the one Skylor considered more fun—that is, the one without five o'clock mass. I couldn't really blame him for that. When I was his age, Luke and I sure didn't enjoy going to mass either. Now I felt as if I would give anything in the whole world to hear my mom sing in our old church choir just one more time.

For this week's outing, I made sure I was prepared. I went to the convenience store and bought a variety of party snacks to bring with me. I even visited the LCBO earlier in the afternoon so that I would have something to contribute. Although Willie and Isabelle constantly assured me that I did not need and that I was welcome to anything they had, I did not want to be a

116

moocher. I picked up two cases of beer and a bottle of Baileys to bring to the log cabin.

"Going to the hoedown on the river tonight, are you?" The man behind the counter looked ancient and half-asleep, and his words came out in a lazy drawl.

"I am indeed."

He nodded approvingly. "Should be a nice clear night, for sure. Cold, mind you. Awful cold. That goes without saying up here in this neck of the woods."

"It's the coldest place I've ever stayed for any length of time," I agreed.

"You'll need a few snorts to warm you up, that's for sure." He bent over the counter and looked at me more keenly. "You'll be that girl detective from down Toronto-way, I'm guessing."

I admitted that I was.

"I think they're crazy to think there's anything to find out so long after that boy died," he said frankly. "Tell you the truth, I don't think there was anything to find out at all. But that mom is determined, I've heard. Shame it was, no two ways about it. Anytime a young person dies, it's a goddamned shame, if you ask me. I'll tell you something, young lady," he stuck a bony finger out at me with assertion, "there was a time when as the guy who ran the liquor store, I knew everything that was going on everywhere. Yes, indeed. If folks were having a hard time, they'd come in a little more often and they'd explain why—you know, so I wouldn't think they were turning into raving drunks or something. And usually we'd get to talking, and they'd bend my ear a little about this or that. It'd be the usual—you know, kids, and money problems and whether the better half was staying faithful. Folks knew I could keep my mouth shut, and I didn't pass anything on to anyone else. I liked to think that I was doing a service, so to speak."

"Why don't you feel like that anymore?"

He sighed deeply. "I do, sometimes. But lots of times, people just buy that gut rot that Ale Murphy calls wine, and they can get it a lot cheaper than I can sell it for, so they don't come in here as much."

"Oh, I see."

"It's not just here, of course. All over the place you can find those little businesses where you make and bottle your own wine."

"Yes, I've seen them."

"It's not just wine, either. Beer, too. Although Ale hasn't gotten into that as yet. Give him time, I say," the man predicted darkly. "They don't call him Ale for nothing."

It certainly did seem to be the drink of choice, I had to admit as I looked around the people clustered at the frozen river's edge. I was glad that I had stopped at the liquor store, though. At least I felt a part of things. I caught sight of Willie and handed her the bottle of Baileys. She accepted it and said that she'd put it away for "later."

."No one will use it tonight," she winked at me. "And sometimes we need it after a long walk in the snow. Not all the time," she added hastily, "but some days, it's just what you need."

I agreed and thought that was probably the reason Ale's wine slid down so nicely. If you didn't have a little something in your veins, you would freeze, rooted right to the ground—or so it felt.

The party was just as happy and colorful and festive as Skylor's picture had prophesied. The kids were a study in constant motion, whirling all over the ice. There were no fewer than three bonfires going, and the sound of chatter and laughter filled the cold air. The smell of hot dogs and roasted chestnuts and marshmallows was prevalent and almost irresistible.

I knew almost everyone here now, and I felt welcomed by all. Even Claude Maindiaux was here, and he was quite friendly toward me. He told me that he'd "spied" me out snowshoeing with the local ladies and was glad that I was "getting to know folks."

"We're a pretty good lot around here. It's a small place, and for the most part, the people are good."

Wow, I thought to myself, *Ale's wine was definitely having a mellowing effect on this Belgian.* I was glad and returned his friendly grin, thinking that he was not bad-looking for a man of over eighty. Maybe this wine had a preserving quality, I reflected. Willie and Quinn and Isabelle didn't look their ages either.

The thing that impressed me the very most was the magnificent sky. I could not have ever imagined a night sky of such brilliance and luminousness. The stars were so bright and clear that it felt as if a person could reach up and pluck one out of the velvet darkness. That night there were vestiges of the northern lights—ribbons of color dancing and shining as if they had a life of their own.

Skylor joined me as I gazed up, shuddering in the circle of warmth provided by one of the bonfires.

"It's amazing." I said, sweeping my arm across the vast expanse.

"I love it too," he agreed. "Sometimes I think I like the winter sky more than the summer one, even though it's so cold out. It seems clearer somehow."

He proceeded to point out the North Star, the Big Dipper, and Orion to me. I hadn't thought of any of these since I learned about them in grade school. Skylor was surprisingly knowledgeable, and I told him so.

He shrugged. "It's because I'm interested in them, at least that's what my teacher says. If I'm not interested, I just don't seem to be able to learn at all."

"I think that we're all a little bit that way, Skylor. I know I am."

At that moment, the train whistle blared loudly into the dark winter night, piercing and penetrating the noise of the crowd. Skylor cast his eyes down and seemed to withdraw almost imperceptibly. I had noticed this reaction before, when he had been walking home with Fiona, but I had absolutely no idea what it meant.

"Wow, that train whistle sure is loud," I commented casually.

Skylor raised his eyes to mine and mumbled that he didn't like that whistle—not at all.

"How come?"

"Oh, I don't know." He was still mumbling and had dropped his eyes again, but I figured by making that comment, he might be open to confidences, and so I persisted.

"You must have a reason, Skylor. Why don't you like it? Is it just too loud?"

He sighed deeply and looked me full in the face, as if making up his mind if he should verbalize his thoughts. "It reminds me of my mother." The words were sad and wistful.

"Your mom?"

I decided then and there that I was not going to betray any information that I had come across. Skylor did not need to know that his mother and her problems were common knowledge. I didn't want him to think that I had been discussing her. I knew that he and Fiona were starting to look upon me as something of a friend, and I wasn't going to destroy this still-fragile bond.

He nodded, and I asked, as lightly as I could, "Where is your mom?"

"I'm not sure really. She's out West."

"That's a long way away, isn't it?"

"Ya. And every time I hear the train whistle, I think about how far away it is. I mean, that train is going out west, you know, Gilly. But I don't think I ever will."

The look in his eyes would melt a heart of stone, but I thought that sympathy would not be a good thing right now. I tried to keep my voice casual. "You never know, Skylor. You never know what's going to happen in the future. I know that I seem old to you, but I'm only twenty-six. I sure didn't think that both of my parents would be dead by now, but they are. I don't know your mom at all, but if I were you, I'd be really glad to have your grandma and Quinn and your Murf friends."

"Oh, I am," he agreed hastily. "But sometimes I think about her, that's all."

"Only natural, I'm sure. Now if I were you, though, and I heard that train whistle, I'd be thinking that I was glad that old train was going out West and I could stay here, with all these great folks." I waved my arm to encompass the lively, colorful crowd.

Skylor followed my gesture with his eyes and then he grinned. "You're right. I am glad to live here. I guess I've been a bit of a baby. I really don't want to leave, ever."

Unexpectedly, he threw his arms around my waist and gave

me a quick, bashful hug before dashing off to join the Murf boys on the ice.

Isabelle was approaching me with a question in her eyes. Before either one of us was able to speak, the sound of the fiddle started up and was joined by a resounding chorus of "Waltzing Matilda." Quinn came over and grabbed her by the arm, and Ale grabbed Willie and they proceeded to waltz up and down the frozen riverbank. Conversation, for the present, was at an end.

They were surprisingly exceptional dancers, all of them, and they kept it up for quite some time, until everyone was breathless and spent. I heard the infamous "Truman Sound Saturday Night," which the kids had previously performed for me. There were quite a few other songs that I was positive I had never heard, and I wasn't sure if they were real songs, or local variations like the "Saturday Night" seemed to be.

I wished that I'd been forewarned and had thought to bring a camcorder or a camera with a movie mode because the dancing was very noteworthy, and I've not seen anything like it before or since. But I wasn't much for cameras, and I never did manage to capture anything on tape, but it doesn't matter really. If I want to remember it, all I have to do is close my eyes and drift away, and I can hear the fiddle and guitar music and visualize the Singing Pines couples, dancing and laughing and colorful, their feet moving almost faster than my eyes could see, their hands joined, and their faces clear and bright in the starry winter nightfall.

18

The next day was Sunday, and I felt a little let down. The day seemed quiet and flat after the joyous activities of last evening. I had absolutely no idea what I was expected to do on such a day. I missed home. I missed my little apartment. I missed my stuff.

I had a nice breakfast, and because it was Sunday, Sadie was not as busy as usual and sat with me for a coffee. I was glad for her company.

"So you were down on the river last night, were you?"

"Yes. It was nice really. Those people can really dance. I was mesmerized just watching them."

"Well, there's not much else to do here, and that's no lie."

"Do you ever go down there on Saturday nights, Sadie?"

She sighed deeply. "We used to, George and I, when we were younger. Now, to tell you the truth, by the time we get the restaurant closed up and cleaned for the week that's coming, I'm too tired to do anything but put my poor, aching old feet up and have a nice cup of tea. George and I like to watch a good hockey game. That's our big Saturday night together."

"Nothing wrong with that. You're a Leafs fan, are you?" I glanced at her sideways, and she grinned. "We both are. Not too many of us true, died-in-the-wool fans left."

I laughed. "My brother is one too. And my dad was. Mom and I always used to tease them because they haven't won for …how long?"

She laughed too. "I've lost count, and that's no lie."

"I got a joke about that on the internet at home. It was about Canadian temperatures, and how we just get so accustomed to colder weather here. I don't remember it all, but the gist of it was that when Americans were wearing winter coats, Canadians were already swimming. And it went on like that until the last comparison, when it said, 'hell freezes over and the Leafs win the Stanley cup.'"

We laughed together.

"I wish I could remember it all. If I'd brought my laptop, I could print it off for you. It's really funny. I think it came from Jeff Foxworthy."

"He is funny, that guy. George and I like him too. I wish all these jokes didn't come on the internet, though. George and I don't have access to it, and we'd have no time to use it if we did. People don't seem to tell jokes anymore. They get passed only on the bloody computers."

I thought that I was, indeed, far from home. Even my mom and my friends' parents have computers and internet connections. It was hard to fathom not having one in this day and age.

"My brother was talking about that not too long ago. He says that people don't tell jokes anymore because they have to be so careful about what is politically correct. All these words that we used to use, we can't use now because they're bound to offend someone."

Sadie sniffed. "Not around here, they're not. You can say whatever you want. There's no one to offend. We're all the same."

I was reflecting on this when old Pete entered the room and nodded his thanks to George, who stopped cleaning the counter-top to pour the Frenchman a cup of coffee.

"Bon jour." He touched his cap politely as he passed us and went to sit at his customary spot by the front window.

We both said good morning, and Sadie added, "Pete's a Leafs fan too, aren't you Pete?"

He nodded his assent and smiled faintly.

"Go Leafs, go!" This came unexpectedly from George, be-hind the counter, and we all laughed.

"My dad used to say that a true fan was someone who cheered for a team whether it ever won or not. He said that he and Luke were true fans and that there was no use in backing another team at his age. He was always a Leafs fan."

"Your dad, my dear, had the right idea. And now I suppose I'd better get back to work. I don't want George thinking he works harder than I do, and that's no lie. What will you do, Gil-lian dear?"

I sighed and said that I wasn't sure, that maybe I'd call my brother.

"Go ahead and use the phone in our office there. It's not busy today. And if you want to, you can take Little Brown Jug out for a little jaunt."

I said yes to both of those suggestions, glad to have a bit of a plan.

I called Luke, and I was immediately homesick from just the sound of his deep, kind voice. Luke was like my dad — rock solid, sensible, and totally dependable. A longing to see him filled me as I heard his voice, and I could feel it welling up in my throat. I struggled to keep my own voice steady. He, of course, was mostly interested in how the "case" was com-ing along.

"I've told you, Luke, I don't think there's too much to find out. I've talked to almost everybody up here, and the general opinion is that the boy just fell and whacked his head."

"Well, that mother of his sure doesn't agree."

"I know, but I can't just make it up, Luke. I don't think it's a big case at all. I think it was just an unlucky accident. Can't I please come home?"

I could hear Luke's sigh as he heard the misery in my voice. "I thought that you were starting to like it up there."

"I am. I really am. But I do still get homesick, you know. Sundays are bad."

"I know."

Luke and I had found Sundays hard since our folks had died. Mom had always wanted us home on Sundays, no matter how old we were. She said that was the day that she missed our dad the most too. And so we had usually contrived to do something together on Sundays, or at least to have a meal together. Now there was only Luke and me, and it was always a lonely day for both of us. We would often have friends in for dinner or to play euchre, or go see a show to keep us busy. There was not too much to keep me busy up here.

"Will you call Barbara Mainwright again?" he asked.

"Do I have to?" I whined. "I can't even stand her voice. She wasn't well-liked up here, you know."

"I can imagine. I don't like hearing from her, either. But she calls the office, and I don't know what to say to her. She is paying us, Gilly."

"I know. I know. I'm going to let her stop paying me and have her let me go home."

"It won't be good for our reputation if we quit in the middle of a job."

"Easy for you to say, you big galoot. You're not the one who can't go home."

"I know, Gilly, but you're getting there, you know. You're into your second week."

"I do like the people, Luke," I said reluctantly. "I just feel hemmed in up here."

"You're used to the urban life, that's all."

"Well, this is quite a stretch, you know. There must be an in-between."

"Have you heard from Sally?"

"Sally Big Boobs?"

"No need to be nasty, Gillian dear."

"I'm not. Even Mom called her that."

"She did not."

"I heard her. Anyways, I haven't heard from her, nor do I want to."

"I thought you were lonely."

"I'm not lonely. The people up here are amazing and very friendly. I'm homesick. It's a different kettle of fish completely."

"Well, you give Barbara Mainwright a call, and I'm going to see if I can come up for a weekend."

"Really?"

"Really. I have to get someone to cover my security shift—Jake said he could do it—not this weekend, but the one after."

"Two weeks from now, you mean?"

"Yes."

"It sounds like a long time."

"Time flies, Gilly."

"Actually," I brightened, "that will be good because every two weeks, they have a fiddle player and a guitar player down at the river, and they all dance and stuff, Luke. It's amazing to watch."

He laughed. "Sounds good. Hang in there. It will be here before you know it."

I was considerably cheered by the thought of Luke's visit, calculating that I would be almost done with my stint here by that time. My spirits were so lifted that I broke down and called the Mainwrights' number on Sadie's big, obsolete telephone.

Mr. Mainwright answered with the welcome news that Barbara was out doing some early Christmas shopping. He was much more pleasant and easier to converse with than his hoity-toity wife.

I gave him a concise summary of my findings (absolutely nothing) and told him that I didn't know whether there was anything at all left to "detect."

"I know, my dear. But it is Barbara's sincere wish that you carry on for the allotted time."

He must have heard the sigh that I couldn't keep behind my lips, and it escaped to travel down the phone cord and miles south.

"I actually enjoyed our time spent in Truman Sound. I found the people among the nicest that I'd ever encountered. Neil Quinn and Reg Barnett—well, he's dead now, of course—and even Ale Murphy was quite friendly to me, to all of us. They say that occupants of small villages are aloof and keep to themselves, but I don't think that's true of the Truman people."

"No, I agree. They have all been very welcoming to me," I said.

"Barbara, of course, didn't cotton to them as much. She's a real city girl."

"Not too much shopping or bright lights around here," I agreed.

"You know, Miss Cooper," he said in a serious tone, "I don't want you to think that Barbara is accusing someone up there of actually killing Ryan. It's more that she just wants to know what really happened. It's awful, not knowing." His tone was sad now. "You see, by the time they found him, it was sixteen hours or so after he died, and anything could have happened. Sometimes you don't ever find out, I guess. Do you remember that case about fifteen years ago, just north of Orillia? A fourteen-year-old girl was found dead in her back yard by a friend?"

"Vaguely. But that was a totally different situation, I think."

"Of course. But I'm just saying that sometimes there are a lot of things that are never brought to light—things about the people who live around there that could have helped when looking at the whole situation. There are lots of different ways of perceiving these things."

I personally thought that this man had been watching too many *CSI* shows, or maybe he'd been living with his horrible wife for too many years. As far as I could see, there was only one way of looking at Ryan's death, and that was to look at the facts. Many people had done this, including those of the long arm of

the law, and the facts seemed to be indisputable. I said as much
to Mr. Mainwright.

"It's just that I feel as if I've exhausted all of the possibili-
ties. I don't know where else to look."

"Just keep detecting, Miss Cooper. Sally said that you were
very good at your job and would not be inclined to give up until
you had some kind of an answer."

"That's just it, Mr. Mainwright. I don't know if there are any
more answers to be found. But I'll keep looking."

I thought, as I rang off, that after all, maybe I preferred Barbara's out-and-out nastiness to this man's passive-aggressive hints.

19

I was sitting in Sadie's office, mentally going over the last two conversations, when Little Brown Jug came in and nuzzled up against me. I laughed and scratched his back.

"Do you want out of here?" I asked him. "Come on."

I bundled up, musing that I didn't think that I'd ever get used to the crippling cold temperatures. Sadie's old-fashioned thermometer, which hung from the back door of the restaurant, read minus twenty-five. I wondered how these people survived when January and February swept over their lives. Thankfully, I would be home by then. Maybe I would visit again in the summertime, when the climate would be more bearable.

The Little Brown Jug was shivering, too. He didn't have a lot of hair, and his fat, squat body hung quite low to the ground. After he peed in the snowbank, he looked at me as if to ask me what was wrong with my head to be out on such a day. I wondered myself and was turning around when I felt a snowball go whizzing by, an occupational hazard of staying in this little place. This time, though, I was not surprised to find out that the throwers of the snowballs were none other than Skylor and Fiona—the usual suspects, it seemed.

"Aren't you guys cold?" I asked, shivering.

They had wound scarves haphazardly around their heads, but their ears and much of their faces were reddened and glowing.

"Nah! We're not cold. What are you going to do when winter comes?"

I thought it would be rude to say that I would be home, where the temperatures were at least temperate enough to sustain life, so I just laughed and said that even the Little Brown Jug was cold.

"That's because he doesn't move around enough," Skylor observed, probably correctly.

"Anyways, do you want to come over? Nanabelle thought you might be lonesome. She says that Sunday is a day that people who are away from home could get homesick."

"Your nana is very insightful."

"If that means that she understands people, you're right. Sometimes she knows what I'm thinking even before I do, if you know what I mean," he added, blushing that sweet, shy blush of his that I was starting to be quite fond of.

"Ya, she's pretty smart," Fiona agreed. "You sure can't put anything over on her, even though she's kind of old. We've tried too, haven't we, Skylor?"

"Nothing too awful, I hope," I said mildly.

"Oh, no." Skylor shook his head. "I love Nana. I really do. I loved Papa too. I miss him lots, even now."

"He was a nice man, for sure. He'd always tell Sky and me jokes, and sometimes Aunty Izzy would think they weren't appropriate. But he didn't mind. He and Quinn used to laugh and joke about all kinds of things. They were the best of friends. I imagine Quinn misses him too."

"He does. He's told me so before. You know what they used to do, Gilly? Their houses are right across from each other, except for the river in between, and they used to signal each other with their flashlights, using Morse code. That's a series of dots and dashes—or when you use light, it's short and long flashes."

"I've heard of it," I said. "People don't use it much anymore."

"Well, that's just it." Skylor explained earnestly. "But if your friend knows it—like Quinn and Papa—you can communicate just between yourselves. It's neat, really. It was first used by the German people in 1905. The one that Papa said they used the most was the signal for SOS. Do you know what it stands for?"

"I think it stands for 'save our souls,' doesn't it? But I don't know the code for it."

"It does. And the code is three short, three long, and three short. It can be stamped in the snow or written in the sand, and it reads the same way upside down as it does right side up."

"Well, I didn't know all that," I said and was impressed all over again at the uniqueness of the knowledge of these kids who seemed so knowledgeable in some ways and yet so naïve in others.

They were tumbling over each other in the snowbanks now, and I guessed that was why they didn't seem to feel the cold—they were always moving.

"I better get this fat little fellow back to Sadie's before he freezes his legs off."

"Then will you come over?" Skylor asked.

I hesitated.

"Please. It's fun when you're around."

"Well, thank you." I was touched by his admiration, maybe because I quite admired him too. "But are you sure I wouldn't be imposing?"

They both groaned.

"We told you," Fiona said with a show of elaborate patience at my lack of understanding, "that's not how it is. We're glad to have you. We don't have that many new people around."

"Oh, I see. I'm a novelty, am I?"

They both laughed and said together, "Exactly," which made them laugh more.

"All right then, if you're sure."

"We're sure."

So I took the poor frozen dogsicle inside to thaw out at Sadie's and headed down to Singing Pines. It did seem as if Isabelle was expecting me and was very pleased that I'd come. She said that Ale and one of the garage fellows were attending some sports event in Timmins with the older Murphy boys, while Camille was shopping with her girlfriends. That left Willie and Fiona and Shay and Skylor, so they were going to have a little gathering of their own—although I was beginning to realize that they didn't need much of an excuse for that.

Isabelle was stirring a big pot of some unknown substance. It smelled like peanut butter and oatmeal, but it looked suspiciously like bird food.

She grinned at my quizzical expression. "It probably doesn't look like anything you've ever seen before, Gillian, does it?"

I admitted that it did not.

"Every week, I mix up a batch of suet for the birds and just throw in whatever I have leftover from the week. They get so cold, the poor things."

"How do you know where to start?"

"I have a recipe of sorts, but I usually stray from it quite a bit. I hate to waste things, so I throw lots of odd stuff in. Reg used to say that a recipe was only a guideline."

I laughed. "That's how I cook. I follow the recipe very loosely. Mom used to be able to just figure it out in her head, but I'm not always successful at doing that. I guess it takes practice. I should write your bird food recipe down and use it when I get home. Mom has a bunch of bird feeders around the store. It's used to be a craft shop, so most people that visited it are into birds and stuff like that. A lot of them were friends with our mom. Luke and I still have them hanging up and we still fill them now and then, but not as religiously as she did."

Isabelle smiled and slid the recipe across the table at me, along with a pen and piece of paper. I wrote:

one cup peanut butter
one cup lard
two cups cornmeal
two cups oatmeal
one cup flour
raisins, sunflower seeds, nuts, or birdseeds
Skylor's leftover crusts or leftovers in general
Melt lard and peanut butter over low heat until melt-
ed. Mix in dry ingredients. Spread into pan to cool then
cut into squares or pour into small containers to cool.
Garnish Mr. Chuck Inukshuk accordingly.

I laughed as I wrote the recipe out verbatim, in the back of my mind thinking that I'd probably never use it. Luke and I seemed to have enough trouble buying and filling the bird feeders at the shop, let alone making a special mix for them. I marveled at Isabelle doing this every week. Even though her finances were probably quite strained, she still made sure she had the supplies and time to feed her feathered friends. I liked her so much.

And so the Sunday passed in a very quiet, pleasant manner. Apparently, when there was some time to spare (like today) and Willie, Belle, Skylor, and Fiona were present, the plan was to watch the TV series *Lost*. Quinn had supplied a DVD of the first season, which had been enough to hook the aforementioned crew, and now they were working their way through the second. I had watched bits and pieces of the show and knew the general story line, and nothing would do but that I join them. They had popped popcorn in the fireplace, and everyone lined up with pillows and velour blankets to snuggle up in.

Quinn arrived just in time to stoke the fire and get the popcorn popping properly. This, it seemed, was his area of expertise. Isabelle had a set of four pokers for the fireplace, which were like nothing I had ever seen. The handles of them were fashioned into the heads of forest animals—a moose, a deer, a wolf, and a bear. Like everything else in her unique log cabin, they seemed to be works of art.

"Someone Reg knew made them for him," Isabelle explained. "He was a blacksmith, and Reg had fixed a few things for him at no charge when he was down on his luck, so this fellow made them for Reg by way of saying 'thank you.'"

"I've never seen anything like them," I said. "Why, this weighs a ton. I can barely lift it."

Quinn laughed. "They're one of a kind, all right. Do you like popcorn, Gillian Cooper?"

"I do."

"You've never had it unless you've had it popped in the fireplace. It's got a real sweet taste to it."

"We pretend we're camping," Fiona said from the confines of her blanket.

Willie sniffed. "Camping with a lovely, warm fireplace and a TV. Really roughing it, you two are."

"Do you know the story of *Lost*, Gillian?" Skylor asked. "We've been following it, and we want to get through this series because someone might get series three for Christmas. You never know."

It was a funny twist of fate that the next episode to be watched (after much debating and arguing about where they left off last Sunday) turned out to be episode nineteen, which was entitled "SOS." The kids paused the player after finding the appropriate spot, and the popcorn was attended to by Isabelle. The administrations of such were delicious toppings, and I never did discover the exact nature of them. But I've never had popcorn like it since. It was passed around in big striped bowls, and a lot of it ended up adorning the wood floor, but Isabelle didn't seem to mind. She said that hard wood floors were easy to sweep up.

Meanwhile, Skylor and Fiona were relating to Quinn how they had explained to me all about the origin of the "SOS" term and how it could be used.

"They did, indeed," I said. "They know lots of things, these two."

"Useless information," Willie remarked, ruffling Fiona's auburn hair. "Her head's full of it, so it is."

"Well, I remember when Papa used to do the SOS signal from our window over to Quinn's," Skylor declared.

Right then, Quinn lifted his head from the fire he was poking about at, and he and Isabelle exchanged a look. I had no idea what it signified, but I felt quite sure it was important. I couldn't figure out what, if anything, was going on between these two.

"In spite of the fact that we've always had a working phone line," was Isabelle's comment, said in a tone which seemed to be deliberately light.

"Ah, but you miss the mystery that way, my dear friend, Belle. It's exciting to use the old distress signal."

Isabelle shook her head.. "Probably the biggest distress was that one of you was out of beer or something."

"You never know. If the good old hockey game was on, that would be a distressful situation, to be sure."

Willie and I laughed, but I couldn't help feeling that there were a lot of unspoken words in the air.

We settled down to watch the episode in which Bernard wanted to use the SOS signal, and it was confirmed that Skylor and Fiona were right in their definition of the signal—three short and three long and three short again.

After that, the big discussion was whether the character of Kate should be with Jack or Sawyer. Skylor and Isabelle liked Jack, but Quinn and Willie thought that Sawyer was more exciting. I was neutral, just letting all of the laughter and debate float around me, and I realized I wasn't homesick anymore. I felt quite happy, really, looking forward to my brother's visit.

Isabelle had filled the crockpot with chili and the oven with homemade biscuits, both of which smelled divine. It was just assumed that I would stay and eat and watch a few more episodes.

I did this with pleasure and had to admit that the story line was quite interesting once you got involved in it a little.

Quinn almost started a big uproar when he referred to their beloved series as a "glorified *Gilligan's Island*," but when Isabelle remarked dryly that she noticed that he, himself, didn't seem to mind following the story, he chuckled and admitted that she was right.

When the night was wrapped up and we were preparing to head back home Skylor slipped outside with us and plugged in the Christmas lights, which I had seen Isabelle and Quinn fiddling around with earlier. There must have been two thousand of them, and they engulfed the blue spruces in a glow of red and green. Even Mr. Chuck was outlined in all of his glory. I thought it was magnificent, and I said so.

"Nanabelle thought it was a little early, but I persuaded her. I knew you'd like to see them, Gilly."

I called back my thanks and appreciation as the dark shadows of the Truman night sky embraced me. I walked back to Sadie's with only the now-familiar stars to light my way.

20

The next day was Monday, and I couldn't wrap my head around the fact that this was my second week in Truman Sound. Even more, I didn't hate it here anymore, and there were even parts of it that I was enjoying very much. I shook my head in amazement.

Willie and Isabelle had just taken it for granted that I would be snowshoeing with them every morning, and this warmed the cockles of my heart. I felt very included, and I appreciated the exercise too. I was determined not to forsake my newfound sport when I returned to Newmarket, although finding a sufficient amount of snow to pursue it could well pose a problem. It was hard to imagine such a dilemma up here, where they had so much snow everywhere.

On one of our morning tours, we encountered Quinn, who thought that I should come over for a coffee when I was done with "the girls" because he had not been interviewed by me yet. I felt awkward, having already spent so much time with him at the log cabin, but he insisted that if everyone on the street was supposed to been spoken to, he should be included.

"I," he announced grandly, "am a fountain of information."

This sent Isabelle and Willie into peals of laughter and sent me on my way across the river to Quinn's house. He had the coffeepot on and a plate of Oreos out on the table.

"It's not as cozy as Isabelle's, so we'll have to make do," he said with a broad smile. "I wish I had her fireplace. Reg and some old German guy built it years ago; it's rare to see such workmanship these days. I envy her those pokers too. They're one of a kind."

"They're heavy," I observed. "You could kill somebody with one of those. I couldn't believe the weight of them."

"Yes, indeed. They don't make them like that anymore," Quinn agreed.

"Her place is always warm and cozy," I said. "I love it there."

"I do too," was his simple reply. "Isabelle has done well holding things together since Reg died. It sure hasn't been easy for her. He was a great guy, you know. I miss him something awful. He was my best friend."

"He sure sounds like a nice man. Everyone speaks highly of him."

"Oh, you wouldn't hear a bad word about him, you're right. It's such a bloody shame about their daughter. I'm sure it had a bearing on Reg's dying so young. They say stress is a big cause of lots of illnesses, and he took it all very hard. So did Isabelle, mind you, but I think women are stronger when coping with these things. It tore the heart right out of Reg, and he never got over it."

"That was Skylor's mom, I guess?"

"Yes. And you know, Gillian, she was the nicest little girl that you would ever want to meet. She was pretty too. You can imagine, because Belle's a beauty, even now. You should have seen her when she was younger. No one could hold a candle to her. And Shantelle looks just like her mom—or she did. She looks like an old, shriveled-up lady now."

"That's a shame."

"That's what it is, all right. It's a crying shame. Rose and I could see it for a while, before Reg and Isabelle noticed. I don't know if that was just denial, though. You want so bad to believe that it's not true. Like I said, she was as pretty as a picture, and then she started getting thin. Not a healthy thin, mind you, but a pale, sickening skinniness that you could see was not right. Her teeth were discolored, and her nose was always running, and she'd act strange—really hyper and talking a mile a minute, and then sometimes she'd act as if she didn't even know you.

"Our daughter was about her age, and she was at a gathering that Shantelle also attended, the summer before she went out west. The party was at somebody's house on the other side of Truman, and they had a swimming pool—I don't know why, when we've got such great lakes to swim in all around here, but that's beside the point. Emily, our daughter, said that Shantelle had been with this fellow—the one she ended up leaving town with—and they'd been snorting cocaine. Later on, Shantelle turned around and jumped in the pool. She came up screaming, from the chlorine I suppose."

"Oh, I never thought of that. I guess the inside of her nose would be pretty tender if she was using cocaine."

"Emily said that Shantelle and her boyfriend were just roaring in pain. And their noses were bleeding. It was shortly after that incident that they left. Not a word to Reg or Isabelle. They just left."

"It's very sad."

"It is. I lost my daughter." His voice dropped a little, and his words were heavy. "In a car accident. I miss her every day. But I know that she's not in any danger, not anymore. And she's with her mom now, which is a comfort. Poor Isabelle doesn't know if her girl is alive or dead."

"Drugs are a terrible thing when they get hold of you like that. It's so awful."

"It is. When Shantelle did get in touch with her parents, she was in desperate circumstances. She'd had a baby, and she couldn't look after him. They were living in a broken-down, old car, and she was still taking drugs. Reg wouldn't let Belle go out, so I went with him. I'll never forget the look of her. If I'd passed her on the street, I tell you, I wouldn't have known her. She was skin and bones, and her face looked yellow, and her teeth were half-broken. It was awful. Skylor was two, but he looked like a baby still. He'd been tiny at birth. I guess that a lot of babies born to junkie moms are really small. Reg and I found that out. It makes me sick to think of it. Poor little things are doomed before they're even born. I thought Reg was going to break right down, but he didn't, not then, anyways. He was there to get that boy, and that's what we did. It was awful. Better to have no mom at all, I think. She didn't even give him a second glance—just let him go."

"Maybe she knew that he would be well looked after."

He gave me a sideways glance and shook his fine, grizzled head.

"It wasn't like that, Gillian. She was beyond it. There was a dog scrounging around the car. He was a skinny, diseased-look-ing thing—like them. I asked Shantelle's boyfriend if that was their dog. Want to know what he said?"

"What?"

"He looked at the dog in this vague, stupid way and said that he didn't know. He didn't know if it was his own damned dog. I felt like asking, 'Do you even know if this is your kid?' But I didn't. I knew how much it meant to Reg to get that boy home safe and sound. But it broke him inside. He went and bought a bunch of groceries and left them in that old tin can of a car for them. He wanted to give them money, but we both knew exactly where that would go. Anyways, we got Skylor out of there and fed him and took him home to Truman Sound."

"He's a lucky boy now."

"He is. It saved Isabelle and Reg. It really did. I will never, to my dying day, forget the day we arrived home with him. Isabelle came running outside to see him, and she sank down into the snowbank and held out her arms. Do you know, Gillian, that that boy ran straight into her arms, even though he'd never set eyes on her before in his little life? It was like he knew. He knew he was home and she loved him and he was safe."

I had heard this story from Sadie, and somehow, I could see it in my mind's eye. I could see a little boy who had been neglected and lost knowing, even at his early age, that this was where he was meant to be.

"He's a nice boy. They did a good job with him," I commented. "I've become quite fond of him."

"He likes you too. He told me so. Lots of people talk down to him, I think. He's shy, but he's getting better. I hope he grows a little. I guess that's one of the hazards of taking drugs—kids tend to be small, and some have trouble at school. Skylor has trouble in some ways. In others, he's very smart."

"He's certainly a talented boy," I said, thinking about the portrait of Quinn, which was to be his Christmas gift. "I was telling Isabelle about the Ontario College of Arts in Toronto. It would be great if he could go somewhere like that in the future. He needs to cultivate his gift."

"You're right, of course. I don't know how Isabelle will ever be able to let him go that far away, though."

"Well, not for years and years, of course."

"Even then. She wants so much for him to be safe."

That seemed like a strange choice of words. Surely, Skylor was safe as anyone. Maybe Isabelle was afraid of her daughter's return and her possibly wanting Skylor back. That must be a concern too.

He poured some more coffee and laughed. "Well, we sure as hell haven't done much delving into the Mainwrights, have we? I don't know anything about them, anyways. I knew the dad a little, but you can count on one hand the number of times I'd even seen Ryan. He wasn't my type of kid, really. Too full of himself, though I didn't have anything against him, mind you. It was sad, that's for sure. But I don't have any information that will help in your inquiry."

"Why did you want me over then?" I laughed.

"Well, I didn't want to be left out. Even old Claude got a visit, I heard. It's always nice to share a coffee on a cold day like this."

I stood up to go, and I could see that his window was, indeed, straight across from the windows of the log cabin.

"This is the site of the SOS signals the kids have been talking about, I guess," I observed.

"You got it. We are exactly across from each other—perfect for light signals. It seemed like fun then. Isabelle's right, of course," he sighed as he got to his feet, "our biggest emergency was most likely related to beer or hockey. No need to use the old flare lights anymore. I know some people think that Belle and I are more than friends, but they're dead wrong. We're just great friends who share a large part of our pasts."

"Maybe she'll fall in love again someday," I remarked, more to be the devil's advocate than anything else. "As you say, Quinn, she's still a very good-looking woman."

Quinn smiled, rather sadly, I thought.

"She is indeed, not to mention one of the most genuinely nice people in the world. But I think you're wrong about the other, my little detective girl. Oh, she's in love all right. I know that it sounds really corny, but it's the truth. She fell in love the day that Reg and I brought that little boy home. Her heart belongs to Skylor."

21

It was during one of our snowshoeing mornings that another mystery was revealed to me, this one regarding the circumstances surrounding Isabelle and Quinn the night that Ryan died. Since my visit to Quinn, I kept my ears pricked at the mention of those two names together. In spite of Quinn's last words to me regarding Skylor as the love of Isabelle's life (which I was quite certain was true), I got the impression from Quinn that there was a substantial amount of affection and respect flowing from his side of the Truman River.

We had been talking about the aforementioned night and the events occurring at Isabelle's house, including Quinn's staying the night, ostensibly to take her to the hospital in Timmins early in the morning for bunion surgery.

"I had Skylor, you see," Willie explained, "because Isabelle and Quinn had to leave so early. And we always worry a little about our Belle because she has mitral valve prolapse."

"It's not that bad really. It's just the thought of being put under anesthesia that I find unsettling." She turned to me and said, "I had rheumatic fever when I was a girl, and I've got a bit of valve damage from it. It's called mitral valve prolapse—MVP for short."

"Oh, I think that Fiona and Skylor were trying to explain this to me one day. They used some letters and told me that it was from having strep throat, or something like that."

"It is." Isabelle nodded. "Antibiotics didn't used to be as widely used as they are now. When I was young, if you had an earache or a sore throat, you just kind of toughed it out—especially if you lived a piece away from the doctors and your folks didn't have a car."

"Maybe it was better then," Willie mused. "Now all you hear about is the overuse of antibiotics and how we're getting all these super bugs that are resistant to all of them."

"Yes," I agreed. "They want to be good and sure you need them before they give them to you, that's for sure. It used to be they'd give them out for a bad cold. I can sort of remember that."

"I guess one is as bad as the other. I just know that when I was a kid, rheumatic fever was the biggest cause of heart valve disease. I know several people around my age who had it, and some ended up with big problems and had to have artificial valves put in."

"So it was caused from strep throat?" I asked. "I think that's what Fiona and Skylor were trying to tell me. Skylor says that you always worry when he gets a sore throat."

"That's true," she sighed. "I worry about him anyways, the little scamp. And strep throat doesn't usually go untreated anymore, thank God. The way I understand it is that the rheumatic fever is actually not the infection itself, but the result of an untreated strep infection. It's the strep bug that causes the body to send out antibodies to fight it, and it can attack the tissues of your joints and heart. I remember my joints being all swollen and sore for months. But the main thing is that it can cause your heart valves to swell and leave scarring. It makes it harder for the valves to open and close properly."

"I didn't know any of that. But I can certainly understand why you're concerned about strep throat."

"Oh, they can do a quick test for strep throat now, right in the doctor's office," Willie said. "Honestly, I've never heard of anyone else having it besides my friend Belle here."

"That's the difference in our ages, my dear."

"Well, you're in pretty good shape, Isabelle," I told her. "I'd never know that you have any kind of a heart problem."

"I don't really have much of a problem now. But that's why I do try to exercise and keep going. I don't want to get into a sedentary lifestyle. That seems to be the worst thing for your heart—at least that's what they say now."

I didn't think there was much danger of that and I said so.

We all laughed.

"I don't know. Some days, I think it would be easy."

"What? To be sedentary?"

She shrugged. "Sometimes."

Willie laughed. "You'd go crazy, Isabelle Barnett, and you know it."

"I probably would," she admitted. "I do remember that from when I was a kid. They thought then that it was good for your heart to rest it. I'd have to lie down for days and days, inside or on the porch, and watch the others play. It almost killed me. I've always loved the outdoors. My sister, Barbara Ann, still remembers my crying and crying because I couldn't go hiking and swimming with them."

"Maybe that's why you like to be so busy now."

"Could be. But I'm lucky, really. The only time I ever had any real problems was when I was pregnant—not so much the first time, but the second time, when I was pregnant with Shantelle."

Her voice was matter of fact, but her face looked a little sad, I thought. Or maybe I was just imagining things.

"And that's why we worry about her when she has any kind of surgery."

"Is it dangerous?" I asked.

"Not really. It's just that if I have surgery, I have to take antibiotics beforehand—even if I have a tooth pulled or something like that. It's no big deal, but since I've had Skylor with me, I worry a little more. You know, I have to keep going—I'm all he's got now."

"Oh, Belle," Willie scoffed. "You'll outlive all of us."

"I don't know about that, but I am quite healthy. It's hard not to worry about stuff, though, when you know that they're going to be knocking you out."

"I can understand that."

"That's why Quinn came over. He spent the evening with Skylor and me, and then we took Skylor down to Willie and Ale's because we had to leave so early in the morning. It's a two-hour drive, and I was supposed to be there for seven o'clock. You can never be too sure of the roads around here, either, especially in the winter months."

"And it did snow that night too, as I recall," Willie said.

"That's right. We ended up leaving at about four thirty in the morning, and I remember it was snowing quite a bit. I was glad that Skylor was down at your house."

"Oh, he's no trouble. He's such a polite, shy kid—not like my brood."

But by now I had gotten to know Willie's kids, and I remembered their kindness toward Skylor, especially Fiona's, of course. I knew how cruel some kids could be, and I knew the Murfs were basically a kind bunch. And their manners were quite respectable too. I said as much to Willie, causing her to grin.

"They're all right," she admitted. "But that Skylor is just sweet through and through."

"I have to agree with you there. I've never known a young boy like him."

"He's been through a lot, one way or the other," Isabelle said softly. This was the first time that I'd heard anything about this from her, but she did not elaborate. Maybe someday she would say more. I didn't know why, but I felt so drawn to both of them. I hoped that I could always be a part of their lives. I hoped that we would keep in touch. I wanted to watch the progress he made in his art studies and in his life.

"Well, he's doing just fine, I'd say," Willie said heartily. "He seems to be well-adjusted enough."

"He certainly seems fine to me," I agreed.

We were rounding the corner of our trail and coming to the now-familiar spot where Ryan had died and lain, unobserved, for sixteen hours that fateful, snowy night a year ago now. I always felt a little shiver as we approached this spot, and I thought that my two companions did too.

"That's why I didn't know anything about all the stuff that was going on the night that Ryan died," Isabelle said, confirming my suspicions.

"Because you were in the hospital?"

"Yes. They kept me overnight, just to keep an eye on my heart, and when Quinn drove down to get me the next day, it was all over and done with."

"Quinn was worried about you, as I recall. He has a wee soft spot for you, my dear Belle," Willie said, in a light, teasing voice.

"Well, of course he does," was the matter of fact reply. "We were all such good friends once upon a time. Now there's only Quinn and me left. A good friend like that is worth a lot in life. More than anything."

22

Years later, when I looked back on my stint in Truman Sound, it always surprised me how very easily I slipped into the rhythm and rhyme of the life there. It was totally different from anything that I'd ever experienced before, and yet I fell into it so naturally. Luke's theory, when he came to have one, was that Isabelle was so much like Mom that I immediately felt comfortable with her and her life.

He could have been right, but I think there was more to it than that. I was bewitched by the town, I think—by the concept of a place where everyone knew everyone and people were open and friendly and got together all the time. I felt as if I were living in *The Waltons*, or something like that. I couldn't see outside the confines of the town's borders. I felt engulfed and welcomed. I felt that I could just be there and remain there and be happy. I had gone from the extreme of hating to go, of begging not to have to spend five weeks there, to wanting to settle there and wrestle in the snow with Fiona and Skylor and snowshoe with Willie and Isabelle.

If I were living in a TV episode, it would show me getting up and having coffee with Sadie; saying a jaunty "bon jour" in reply to old Pete's greeting; running through the streets with the Little Brown Jug and Truman, who I'd come to learn truly did belong to the entire town; waving to the folks at the garage and the convenience store and all the Singing Pines residents because I knew each and every one of them and they knew me; helping Willie with Girl Guide assignments; and learning recipes and lots of stories and crafts from Isabelle.

Most of all, it would show my great fondness for Skylor growing and growing. There was something about him that seemed to get to me. I'd never known anyone like him. Perhaps it was because I knew his sad story, but it wasn't just that. There was a quality about him that I could never truly define. It was a gentleness, a kindness, an almost otherworldly quality. Luke would have snorted if I'd ever endeavored to put it into words, but that didn't stop me from feeling it. I felt as if we were close. It seemed absurd because we'd known each other such a short time, but I knew he felt it too. There was something else about Skylor that I found indefinable as well. I could not put my finger on it, but it was as if he were haunted or delicate in some way — as if he was not strong and could not stand up to much, not so much in a physical way, but rather in an emotional one.

When I thought about it, I assumed that this would be from the drugs and tough beginning he'd had in his life. I could hardly bear to think of him as a wee, broken boy-child, living in a run-down car with junkie parents. I supposed it happened more than I'd like to imagine, but I hadn't, personally, known anyone whose life had run that course. I just couldn't imagine that all the love and talent that was Skylor might have never come to be if he hadn't been rescued by his grandparents.

"When you live this far up north, you learn to drive between the snowflakes" was a common saying of George's, but

I thought it was true of walking as well. If you didn't walk between the snowflakes, then you'd just never go outside. The
fierce, constant below-zero temperatures alone could keep you
housebound. In my neighborhood at home, if it was this cold or
snowy, the streets shut down and people did not travel unless
they really had to. Up here, a person wouldn't go anywhere if
that were true. They existed in a world full of frigid weather and
unending snow and difficult roads. No wonder Ale Murphy did
so well with his homemade wine. It certainly helped to warm the
ice in your veins.

"Keep the rubber side down and the shiny side up," Sadie
would call out gaily to customers who left to travel the snow-
covered roads.

Maybe the reason I got so attached to the village folks was
because I didn't drive too much during my stay there. At first,
I was wary of the roads because they seemed so isolated and
uncertain, but after a while, there really seemed nowhere to go.
I was content to spend evenings at the old log cabin, watching
the next episode of *Lost* or helping Isabelle sort out fabric for
her beautiful quilts. Somehow, this was starting to suit me much
more than running the roads. Luke was astonished when I said
something like this to him. I had always been a social, outgoing
girl, and if anything was doing in the evenings, then I was doing
it, given the opportunity. He couldn't believe that I was spending
so much time, calmly and contentedly, with the Truman folks.

"You'll see when you come up," I tried to explain to him.
"It's restful, Luke. It's kind of nice and homey."

"I think you've lost your mind, my dear sis. Don't get me
wrong—I'm glad you're not chomping at the bit to get back. I
hope you're all right, that's all. None of it quite sounds like you."

"It's nice here, Luke. That's all. It's just nice here. You'll see."

"Well, as long as you're okay, I'm happy and Barbara Mainwright is happy. Have you talked to her lately, Gill?"

"I called her last week, but they were both out, so I left a
message. But I've told both of them several times now that
there doesn't seem to be much more to find out, and they both

urged me to stay here, just in case. So I'm staying here, and I'm enjoying myself."

"Can't blame you there, Gilly girl."

"I can't wait to see you though, Lucas. I really do miss you. I'm glad you're going to make it."

"I am too. I do miss you too, you know. Not looking forward to the hellish drive, but what can I do?"

"I know. It is awfully long. It's going to take up most of your time off, I guess."

"Can't be helped. Anyways, it'll look good to the Mainwrights that we both visited the village. Have you heard from Sally?"

"No, I haven't. Oh God, Luke, you're not going to see her when you come up are you? That would spoil our time together."

"Come on, Gilly, it's not that bad."

"It is that bad, Luke. She wouldn't even belong here."

"That's not nice, Gill. What would Mom say?"

"Leave Mom out of it. She didn't like Sally's big boobs any more than I did. And I didn't mean people wouldn't like her, but that she wouldn't like them. It's just not her type of place, that's all."

"Why? Because everybody has regular-sized boobs?" he asked lightly, and I laughed.

"Oh, Luke, I just want you to come and visit and see everyone without her. I have so much to show you and so many people for you to meet."

"I know, I know. Don't worry about it. I'll work it out. I can't get over how attached to these people you've gotten in a such a short time."

"You'll see when you meet them," I said softly. "It's a different world up here."

"Well, I hope I like them half as much as you do," he said with a laugh as he rang off.

I reflected on all of this as I started the now-familiar ritual of donning scarf, hat, mittens, coat, and boots to wend my way down to the log cabin. I laughed as I thought to myself that I would be "wending my way." This was an expression of Isabelle's, which I'd never heard used before and was now part of my vocabulary.

As I headed north down the road, it occurred to me that from my perspective, Truman Sound had developed into a place that was much more about the Barnetts than it was about the Mainwrights. It was bizarre and not intentional, but it had certainly turned out that way. I had fallen into the pattern of their lives with comfort and ease. No mystery there: I was just loving it, that was all.

23

Wednesdays, it seemed, were the nights that there were hockey games in neighboring towns ("neighboring" meaning two hours' drive away), and the Murphys liked to attend these when they could. One such night I was invited along, but I declined, not fancying the long, snowy trip and not being a great hockey fan, although I did always want the Leafs to win, but that was only out of respect for my dad.

Skylor liked to go when Isabelle permitted him, and on one of these evenings when he got the go-ahead, Isabelle asked me over. I hoped that she wasn't just being polite because I had expressed an interest, on various occasions, regarding her work shop with its fabrics and scrapbook supplies.

That, in itself, was not too much of a mystery. It was because it reminded me of my mom, plain and simple. I had always liked to be at the store when she was there with all the different woman whom she knew from out and about. It made me feel secure, somehow. Probably that's why Luke and I maintained the store in some semblance or other, although we hadn't ever voiced this to each other. It was more of a feeling.

I was delighted to be taken upstairs into Isabelle's realm of handiwork. I looked at all of her devices for cropping photos and making frames and circles around them. I was familiar with most of them and said so. Mom had used many of these gadgets. I was so glad now that she'd put our photos together and we had the written accounts and photo memories of our cousins and uncles and grandparents—but most of all, of her and Dad.

I said this to Isabelle. "I used to think my mom was nuts to do all this work on pictures and writing things down and all that. Now I don't know what we would have done if she hadn't. You don't remember things exactly as they happen when you're a kid, so Luke and I are lucky—we can just open up one of the books she made, and there are all our memories intact. It's wonderful, really. Skylor's lucky. He may not know it now, but he will someday."

Isabelle turned and pulled down a worn scrapbook from the top shelf. Wordlessly, she handed it to me to look at. The cover was pink and "one-of-a-kind-you" was written beneath a photo of a beautiful young girl. Her features were fine and sweet, and her eyes were big and blue. I realized suddenly that this was surely Shantelle Barnett. I looked up at Isabelle, and she nodded in answer to my unspoken question.

"That's my girl," she said simply, and her smile was the saddest one I'd ever seen on anyone's face. "She's beautiful, isn't she?"

I nodded, noticing her use of the present tense. I'd heard plenty about this girl from Sadie and from Quinn, but never so much as a word from her own mother. I always thought that she would tell me if and when she was good and ready. It seemed that time had arrived. Maybe it would be good for her to talk about her to someone who'd never met her and so was in no position to pass judgment. I hoped so.

The book was, in itself, a work of art. It started with the birth of a baby girl who was loved and cherished beyond anything, if this record was to be believed. And I felt as if I knew Isabelle well enough to know that it could. She was a little pixie of a child with large eyes and a happy smile. She was at the park with her big brother. She was laughing in the spring flowers with a little dog. She was fishing in the boat with her dad. She was walking down the road, holding the hand of a younger, happier Isabelle. I had always thought that Isabelle was a happy woman until I saw these earlier photos, with her unclouded face and the perfect joy and love reflected in her eyes as she looked at her young family. Quinn had been right. She had been a stunningly beautiful young woman.

There were photos of Quinn too. He also was young and cheerful looking, in the company of a dark woman and a girl of Shantelle's age, whom I assumed were his wife and daughter. I strained to remember their names—Rose and Emily, I thought.

Isabelle confirmed this as I pointed to them. "That is Quinn's wife and little girl. They're both dead now. It's so very, very sad. Emily died in a fluke car accident, and Rose never really recovered. They said it was early Alzheimer's, but I never believed that myself. Neither did Reg. It's easy to stick a label on someone if you don't know them. I think she just never got over Emily's death, and it made her crawl more and more into a shell. Reg and I would go over to visit her, and she wouldn't even get out of bed. It was so sad for Quinn too. It's like he lost them both at once. She ended up in a nursing home at quite a young age, and then she got so she wouldn't even talk. She started to get pneumonia because she wouldn't get out of bed, and she'd aspirate when she ate. Quinn called it 'garbage pneumonia' because if she ate at all, it would end up in her lungs and eventually it killed her. It was sad, but it was like she had already gone before she actually died." She sighed and shook her head.

"It's still nice to have pictures of her," I said gently, "so you can remember how she was."

"I suppose. Most of the time, I can hardly bear to look at them. I never take them out on my own—not so much Rose and Emily, although that's hard enough." Very softly, she added, "But the ones of Shantelle really rip the heart out of me. I miss Reg, of course, I do, but I know he's at peace. My girl, though, I don't know if she'll ever find peace on this earth. Dear God, I don't know if she's even still alive."

"That's so sad," I said cautiously, unsure of how much to say. I didn't want Isabelle to think that I'd been gossiping about her and her daughter. It hadn't been like that. I'd not heard one malicious word about them, only words of regret at how things had turned out.

"It's not the pain in itself so much," she said this almost to herself. "It's the possibility of the pain never, ever going away completely. If I miss Greg, I can just pick up the phone and call him. I wish he weren't so far away, but that's life. But my girl—oh, my dear girl—sometimes I feel absolutely starved for her. We got along so well when she was young. We'd go for walks and to the show, and we'd go shopping. We'd go to Timmins and even North Bay, and once we went all the way to Toronto to see *Showboat*, the musical. Most of the time I'm all right, but sometimes I miss her so much I think my heart will break right in two. And I can't just call her up on the phone. I don't know where she is."

The words were filled with a great sadness. My mom and I had been friends like that, and I knew what a loss it was and what a hole losing someone created. This was a different kind of death, though.

"I know you've probably heard things. It's such a small place. She was a wonderful little girl, though, Gilly, just an amazing child. And we all loved her so much. Maybe we loved her too much. I don't know. But there's not one day that goes by that I don't think of her and send up a prayer for her. I think that at least if I can say a prayer for her, it's something, you know. It's all I can do, really."

"My mom always believed that saying prayers for people helped them on their way when you couldn't do anything else. I've heard her say that a million times." I was not so sure that I believed it myself, but this didn't seem exactly the moment to mention that.

"I believe that too. It used to make me so sad, but now when I think of these scrapbooks, I try not to feel that way. I try to think that we had those good times—they're right here, in between these pages. And no matter what else happens, they are here. Nothing can take away these memories. And if Shantelle never makes her way home to claim them, then they can be Skylor's. Maybe the only reward that I'll get out of all of this is Skylor. But then it will still be more than worth it."

"He's a wonderful boy." At least I was on certain ground here. "And so talented."

"Yes. Reg and I were happy every day since he came. He made our lives complete again.

When you have children, their names are etched on your heart forever. That's just the way it is. We have a son too. I'll show you his scrapbook. He's a very successful computer analyst in North Carolina. It doesn't make sense, does it? I mean, how you can raise two children exactly the same and they turn out so very differently. Reg always said that Shantelle was very easily led and that's what got her into trouble. I think that he was likely right about that. She was a sunny-natured little thing, and she wanted everybody to like her. I just think she lost her way, that's all.

I know that when Reg and Quinn went out West to get Skylor, she was thin and her teeth were rotten and her nose was bad. Quinn doesn't think that I know that, but Reg told me one night before he died. We cried together over it. But then we had Skylor, and we lived for him, you see. I miss Reg so much. He was such a good grandpa to Skylor too. Sometimes, Gillian my dear, life does not seem particularly fair."

This seemed like an understatement to me, but Isabelle smiled ruefully.

"Come on. Let's go downstairs and sit by the fire and have a little taste of Ale's wine. I'll show you all the photos of the 'olden days,' as Skylor calls them. Maybe we'll put the next episode of *Lost* on, and we can watch it together. When the others come in we can watch it over again with them and pretend we're psychic, or 'side kick,' as Fiona used to call it. We can pretend that we already know what's going to happen."

I was gathering up the scrapbooks and looked up at her in astonishment.

She laughed. "I'm only kidding. I couldn't go through with it anyways. I'm not good enough at acting."

"One of my dearest memories," she continued as we busied ourselves tidying things up, "is when Skylor first came to us. It took him a little while to feel safe and warm at night, and often he would wake up and crawl in with Reg and me. We didn't care. We liked the feeling that he was right there between us, and we could reach out and touch his sweet little body. Anyways, one night he got into bed with us in the middle of the night, and he was babbling on and on about something. We were half asleep, and I stroked his head for a minute and said, 'Okay, honey, now you go back to sleep until morning.' He lifted his little head up and looked right at me and said, 'What did you say? Did you say I was precious?'"

I laughed and was glad. I knew that Skylor still felt "precious."

The rest of the evening was spent on a lighter note, and I enjoyed it. I was a true child of my mother, and I loved looking at the old photos and the stories they told. I thought that Skylor was lucky to have such a record of his mother. Perhaps he would someday be able to remember her in a good light—if he remembered her at all.

Later, Isabelle and I walked down to the Murfs' to retrieve Skylor and hear about the hockey game. I fell into step with her stride as easily as I was falling into step with the rhythm of her days. The stars were out in all of their northern glory. I never tired of their brilliant beauty.

"I love the nights here," I told Isabelle as the snow crunched beneath our boots.

"I do too," she agreed. "And every night, when I see the first star, I use it for a wish to keep my girl safe for one more day. After all, she's under that same big sky, somewhere. And if I wish it every night, I'll always be one night ahead of her, and maybe I'll keep her safe until she finds her way home again."

One day at a time, I thought wryly, *like that old AA guy that Luke and I drive around at home. Maybe everyone is just trying to make it through life one day at a time.*

24

Isabelle never mentioned Shantelle to me again, but I some-how felt closer to her after that evening, and in some strange way, closer to Skylor too. I knew that other people had stories just as bad or worse, but somehow, I felt a part of these lives, and this made me feel so much closer to them. Even when I was ly-ing down in my bed at Sadie's for the night, my thoughts would creep unbidden back to the log cabin with the inukshuk and the birds, and to the ethereal boy who resided there with his grand-mother who treasured him so much.

I had almost forgotten about the others on the Singing Pines Road until one day I literally bumped into Megan and Kyle Bloom, dragging their young son on a baby toboggan through the masses of snow. I greeted them out of politeness as I walked by, and the girl caused me to pause as she introduced herself and said (in an echo of Quinn's words) that I had not been along to visit them as of yet.

Then I remembered who they were. And I also realized that they were exactly right. These were the dope-smoking Blooms, and I guess I had sort of written them off after hearing the secondhand stories about them. I was surprised at myself for a moment because it had never been my way to listen to other people's stories and opinions about anyone. This was not a very professional way for a detection girl to act, I reflected. Hercule Poirot would not have been impressed. I reproved myself inwardly and accepted their invitation to come in and have a cup of coffee.

The baby was duly admired and set down in his basket to have a sleep, his cheeks rosy from the cold. I was agreeably surprised to find that they were quite a nice young couple, and I again reprimanded myself. I was grateful that I had not voiced any of my opinions to anyone, even Luke, so I could appear to be quite genuine, if a little absent-minded. After all, there were not that many houses on Singing Pines, and the Blooms did mention that they'd seen me go past theirs any number of times.

I explained that I had started snowshoeing with Willie and Isabelle, and they accepted this. They spoke highly of everyone else on the street, which made me feel guilty again for writing them off as a couple of potheads. To be sure, I'd heard things which were not too complimentary about them, and I'd just accepted those judgments. And now I was hard-pressed to recall who indeed said them. Maybe "Pete and Repeat" at the garage (the name that Ale had dubbed them really did seem to fit). I couldn't even remember their proper names at this exact moment, I thought with momentary panic. Oh dear, maybe my brain was becoming immersed in the thought processes of Truman Sound.

Kyle was coming out of the kitchen and into the tiny sitting room, where I had been seated, with a tray of chocolate chip cookies, and Megan was close behind him with a welcome pot of coffee and mugs when I remembered, with relief, the names

of the two "Newfs": Ian and Shane. I was pleased with myself now and smiled my thanks at the couple, who looked very
young—too young—to be married and have a baby and a home.
In short, they were younger than I was.

"I've seen you at the river the last couple of Saturdays," Megan said, almost shyly. "But I've not spoken to you yet."

"I'm sorry about that. The first time I went, I was just dead
homesick, and Willie Murphy kind of took me under her wing.
Then I guess I continued hanging around with them because I
didn't know anyone else. I did stop to talk to everyone on the
street at one time, but you weren't home, and I never seemed to
make it back."

"Oh, that's all right," Kyle said easily. "Sometimes we go
with Aiden to my folks' to stay overnight for a bit of a break.
They live in New Liskeard, and it's over a two-hour drive away.
So you may have missed us. It gets so monotonous here in the
winter sometimes."

"And it's not even winter," Megan sighed. "Not really. You
have no idea how long the winters are up here, Gillian, especially when you're cooped up with a baby."

"I can't imagine," I replied honestly.

"We've been talking about moving back to New Liskeard,"
Kyle said. "I work for the township here. It's busy in the summer, but dead-slow after October. A lot of work up here is strictly
seasonal. Megan is from North Bay, and it would make our lives
easier all around to be closer to our families. I'm drawing unem-
ployment now, but my uncle is looking around for something for
me down there. I'm not afraid to work."

These last words were uttered defiantly, and I wondered if
he felt some of the town's disapproval weighing on him. I might
smoke a lot of dope too, I reflected, if I weren't working and was
living in such isolated circumstances. I hadn't actually smelled
anything suspicious in their house, though, and the baby seemed
well-cared for. Maybe they just took a toke or two to keep themselves on an even keel. It had never been my way, but I knew
some kids for whom it was.

The coffee was black and strong and felt good in my veins after the chill of the afternoon air. We chatted a little, and I found this couple to be less inclined to gossip than anyone else I'd encountered thus far. They spoke highly of both the Barnetts and the Murphys, although they did say they couldn't imagine having five kids—it was lots of work looking after just one.

"You're actually here about Ryan Mainwright, though, aren't you?" Kyle asked eventually. "That's what we heard via the grapevine."

"That is true," I admitted. "So far I've unearthed exactly nothing, but it is making his parents feel better that I am up here trying." I put up both my palms upward. "So I keep trying."

"It would be awful," Megan said, in sympathy. "We've had Aiden for only nine months, but I can't imagine our lives if anything ever happened to him." She gazed with love at the woven basket by her feet, where the object of her affection was snoozing unconcernedly.

"I can't either," Kyle agreed. "But I hope that Aiden doesn't grow up to be too much like that Ryan."

"You didn't like him?"

"He wasn't too likeable. He was stuck-up and arrogant and thought he was way better than us small-town hicks. He wasn't above taking a pull on some weed when he wanted to, though. He wasn't too good for that."

I was unsure what comment to make and so decided (wisely, I thought) to make none.

Megan looked uncomfortable, but she, too, made no comment.

"He was a good-looking son of a bitch," Kyle continued. "But he damned well knew it. I don't think I've ever met a young kid so goddamned sure of himself. He always seemed to have a following running along behind him."

"That's actually what I wanted to say to you," Megan seemed happy to have something constructive to contribute. "We were probably the last people around to see him before he died that night."

My ears pricked up at that, and I was starting to feel a little bit interested.

"It's true," Kyle confirmed. "It was Halloween, and we had been talking about how many kids we'd get, besides the Murfs, of course, and we were outside trying to get our pumpkin to stay lit. It's so bloody cold and windy up here, even then. Winter starts early here."

I nodded but said nothing, and eventually Megan took up the thread of the story. "We just really noticed it because, like Kyle says, Ryan always seemed to have a whole whack of kids trailing behind him or with him."

"He was never alone, anyways."

"That's right. It was the first time ..."

"And the last."

"Yes, and the last that we ever saw him by himself."

They were both telling the story by now, and I listened, trying to follow along to see if there was anything significant to be gleaned from any of it.

"He was hurrying a little. You know, he was kind of hunched over, as if he didn't really want to be seen."

I wondered how much of this was hindsight on their part.

"We mentioned it at the time—to each other—that he seemed to be acting a little weird, out of character, and we wondered if he was meeting someone. He didn't look up or wave or anything. Sometimes he would stop in ..."

For a quick smoke, I wondered.

"But that night, he just kept on going."

"Did you tell the police that?" I asked.

"Oh, yes," Megan said eagerly. "We did, but they didn't think anything of it. It doesn't sound like much if you didn't know him."

"But if you knew him, like we did, it seemed very odd behavior. Not that we think it really means much of anything."

"But we thought we'd let you know."

"And now when you see us on the Saturday nights by the river, you'll recognize us." Megan said this a little wistfully, and I thought that she, like myself, was a long way from home.

I left them with thanks and promises to meet again, and as I headed down their driveway, I reflected how ironic it was that the one house on the street that I had not approached on my own may well be the only one to have any information about the fateful Halloween night in question. I just had no idea on earth what, if anything, I was to do with it.

25

My beloved brother came in time for the next big party at Truman Sound—one featuring Haven McPhee on the fiddle and Ale Murphy on the guitar. I was so happy to see him that I surprised myself by throwing my arms around his waist and hugging him. We were not really a demonstrative a lot, he and I. My mother had been the sentimental one, the one with the hugs and kisses and "I love yous." Luke and I had always understood more or less that we were fond of each other, but like most siblings, did not feel the constant need to express this verbally. But when I saw him pull up to Sadie's in his big black truck, I was filled with love for him and a longing for home.

He was surprised by my reaction, too, but returned my hug with affection as he looked around at the small village bearing the name of Truman Sound. Maybe he felt guilty for exiling me here for five long weeks just for the sake of the agency's reputation, not to mention cold hard cash.

"Who is the Mighty Quinn?" he asked.

I laughed as I explained, and I reflected that it seemed like months instead of weeks since I had pulled in here and asked the same question. I felt so at home here. I couldn't imagine not knowing these people.

I was proud of my tall, handsome brother, and I was happy to introduce him to everyone. Luke had always exuded an easy, friendly air, and people seemed to automatically like him.

We sat at Sadie's and drank coffee and ate her delicious scones and caught up on all the news from both sides.

"People seem to like you just fine, it seems," he observed as various folks came and went and greeted me and asked if I was going to be attending the river party tonight.

"I'm very likeable. Did you forget?"

"No, of course I didn't. I gotta hand it to you, Gilly, I really didn't think that you'd stick it out this long."

"You didn't? Well, what choice did I have?"

He laughed. "We could have turned down the job, I guess. But that wouldn't be very good for our reputation. The Mainwrights are very happy that you've made such an effort, you know."

This last was said on a more serious note.

I sighed. "I know, Luke, but I really feel like it's all a colossal waste of time for us and money for them. I haven't really found out too much at all since I came here—I mean, I've heard little snippets of stuff but none that would prove anything really suspicious about Ryan's death."

"Not even one clue? A sharp little Miss Marple like yourself? I can't believe it."

"Sometimes there's just nothing to find out. Miss Marple solved her mysteries by comparing the people at the crime scene with people that she knew from her own life."

"So does anyone here remind you of anyone back home?"

"You'll see," I laughed. "You should be able to figure that one out."

"When?"

"Tonight. At the river party."

"Oh, right. Will I meet the Mighty Quinn, too?"

"You will."

"Is he very mighty?"

I considered. "Well, I think that the name came more from attributes other than physical ones."

"I don't get you."

"When I asked that question, Sadie and George told me that he was almost a local hero. It wasn't because of any one spectacular thing, but because he helps the local people. George said that he lost one of his fingers when he was helping a snapping turtle across the road so it wouldn't get hit, and the turtle turned around and snapped his finger off."

Luke shrugged. "He doesn't sound like the sharpest knife in the drawer to me."

"I know. I kind of thought that at first, but he really is a great guy. You'll like him. He goes into Timmins once a week or so and picks up stuff for lots of people who can't get out of the village."

"It sure is small. Not much here. It's hard to believe that people actually exist here."

"I've met a lot of people who have lived up here or around here all their lives, and they wouldn't live anywhere else`."

"Well, you can get used to anything, even hanging, as Dad used to say. It's so isolated. I thought I was never going to get here."

"And yet you sent your little sister up here without a second thought."

"That is not true, Gill, and you know it. And this is good for our reputation, you'll see. The Mainwrights are so impressed, even if you don't find out one single thing."

"I won't."

"It looks so good for us that you made the effort and stuck it out."

"Actually, I'm enjoying it so much now that it doesn't seem like a job at all. Life is quite simple and nice up here. I may just stay."

I was half joking, of course, but my mind had wandered on various occasions to consider the idea of taking up lodging here for at least part of the year. Life in Newmarket was like anywhere else, I supposed. Some days were good. Some were bad. Some were joyful, but not many, really. And some days it was all I could do to keep body and soul together. But life in Truman Sound was a different story completely. There was a general air of peace and harmony. The air was crisp and clear, and the stars were so bright that you could almost pluck them out of the sky, so it seemed. I felt as if I could nestle right in here and stay—not forever, but for a while.

Luke laughed. "You're incorrigible. First I can't get you to come, and now I can't get you to leave."

"Oh, I'll leave, Luke. I miss home, especially now that it's almost December. I feel like I've had my winter already, though."

"We haven't even had snow yet."

"I told you. It's a different world."

"I can see that. Do we have to bring anything to this party, by the way?"

"No, I've got us covered. Ale Murphy brings wine that he makes in his basement, and I bought some chips and stuff at the little general store. I bought you some beer too."

"Thanks, Gill. I'm not much for wine, especially the homemade stuff."

"It's like being in a whole other world, Luke. You'll see what I mean. It's quite beautiful."

"I hope I like it as much as you do. By the way, I talked to Sally."

I groaned and rolled my eyes.

"Is that nice?"

"No. And neither is she."

"What did she ever do to you?"

"I'm thinking that she's coming to Truman Sound to wreck the first visit I've had with my favorite brother in three and a half weeks."

"Well, you would be guessing wrong then. She isn't coming."

"Great."

"She got us this job, Gill. It was good of her to recommend us."

"You, Lucas dear—she recommended you. She doesn't give a rat's ass about me. She thought she could get her tentacles into you while you were away from home and vulnerable."

"I think that you are misjudging her."

"You, my dear brother, do not understand women."

"Maybe." He shrugged. "Anyways, she can't come this weekend because she has to go to a convention in Kapuskasing. But she might call you later on in the week and want to meet for lunch or something."

I groaned again. If Sally Big Boobs called, I would be unavailable to take her call, I decided. I preferred the company of Isabelle and Willie and all the Murfs. I hadn't known them long, but at least they were real people. They were totally different from Sally who was all for show. Maybe I'd linger here a little longer, I thought. I was almost getting used to it.

26

When Luke and I approached the log cabin, the party was well under way. Darkness fell as early as four thirty now that it was almost December and that was a good excuse to get things going.

I brought Luke around to the back of the log cabin, where the blue and white lights were gleaming among the branches of the trees down to the frozen river. The bonfires were blazing, and the air was redolent with roasted wieners and chestnuts. I could see that Luke was impressed.

"You're right, Gill. It is very nice."

"This is nothing yet. Wait 'til the music gets started and you see how these people can dance. You won't believe it. I haven't seen anyone dance like this except on TV."

At that moment, we heard a booming voice come from across the river, and its owner approached the cabin, coming up the river's bank.

"Isabelle! Isabelle! Is-a-bell necessary on a bike?"

It was Quinn, of course. I'd heard him call this play on Isabelle's name before. He was grinning and seemed to have eyes only for Isabelle when she detached herself from the crowd and went down to greet him. I wondered yet again how far their friendship extended. I liked them both so much.

I was happy to introduce Luke to Quinn and Isabelle and Skylor and everyone else in turn. He's just a great guy, and most people like him on sight. He fit right in, and before I knew it, he was engulfed by the crowd, with a glass of homemade wine in his hand and laughter on his lips.

I was totally happy that night. When I think about that night, it is with a feeling of contentment and satisfaction. I had grown fond of all these people, and I was so thrilled to have my big brother there. He was all the family I had left now, and when we were together, I felt whole somehow. I felt at peace.

Just as I had been a novelty when I first came (which I felt had worn off some since), Luke was even more of a novelty now. Fiona and Skylor were amusing him with anecdotes and stories, and he seemed to be genuinely enjoying their company.

Once when I approached the group that had formed around Luke, I could hear Fiona recanting an experience she'd had with Barbara Mainwright. I listened intently at the mention of her name.

Fiona was describing an evening when she had been out for a walk and, listening to her Discman, had earbuds. She was walking along, minding her own business, according to her story, when she encountered Barbara rounding the corner at Singing Pines. At this point in her story, she stopped, and she and Skylor began to giggle uproariously.

"What then?" I asked.

"Well, you see, I didn't know she was there. I thought that I was out all by myself."

"Yes?"

She looked at Skylor and said, between fresh onslaughts of giggles, "I farted. I farted really loud."

"Fiona!" This was from Willie, who was approaching the group behind me.

"Sorry, Mom. But it's true. I didn't know she was there, so I wasn't being rude on purpose. You can't help it if you have to ...you know." She looked around at Skylor for moral support, which she got, of course.

"You can't," he agreed willingly.

I was just as bad as they were because I was laughing too. I could just picture the grand figure of Barbara Mainwright looking down on poor Fiona, who was hastening across the snow, thinking that she was alone.

The fiddle and the guitar started up then, and Luke was able to see the impressive ability of these people when they got their dancing feet going. As usual, Quinn grabbed Isabelle first, and they started to dance and sway up and back down across the frozen ground. I felt as if I could watch it forever. When it seemed as if every single person there was dancing, my brother grabbed me by the arms and whirled me to follow in the path of the others.

"I can't dance," I protested. He was swinging me around so fast that I was gasping.

"Nonsense," he laughed, and he wasn't even out of breath. "Just follow me."

So I did. I didn't have much choice, really. He was a foot taller than me, and he was pulling me along expertly. I was laughing so hard that I could hardly breathe. It was great. I felt totally alive.

By the time the music stopped, the food was ready, and everyone started to eat.

"It sure is cold," Luke observed, "now that we're standing still again. And such a lot of snow. It's as if we're in a whole separate country from Newmarket."

"I know. It's hard to believe we're only seven hours north." "You'll have to come up and visit again in the summer," Isabelle said. "It's quite beautiful."

"Somehow, I can't imagine it in the summer at all. I can't imagine it as anything except a winter town." I laughed and rhymed out loud, "A winter town is Truman Sound."

"The snow is falling all around." Luke took up the thread, as we used to do when we were kids.

"I wish it would all leave the ground," Fiona Murphy piped up, getting into the spirit of the poem.

At that moment, the train whistle pierced through the frigid air and echoed into the darkness. I saw Isabelle glance anxiously at Skylor, and I remembered how the sound of that whistle brought back painful memories of his mom.

But he didn't look sad this time. He raised his head and smiled right into my face and said in his shy manner, "I love to live in Truman Sound."

"Good one," Luke called as the pair ran off to procure another hot dog.

Isabelle came over to me and placed a mittened hand gently on my shoulder. "You are a darling girl," she said warmly and then headed after the teenagers.

"What just happened?" Luke asked. "I feel like I missed something."

"It's nothing, really. It's just that Skylor used to feel sad when he heard the train whistle because it goes out west, and that's where his mom is. I talked to him a little and sort of said that maybe he should think about how lucky he was that the train was leaving and he didn't have to, that he had a great home right here."

"Didn't anyone ever mention that to the kid before? It doesn't seem like rocket science."

"You're right. It isn't. But sometimes it takes a stranger to see things and sort them out for you. Anyways, I get the feeling that he never put it into so many words."

"I guess. Anyways, Miss Marple, if you're going to use the strategy of comparing people here to people you know back home, I know where you can start."

"Where?"

"Isabelle Barnett."

"Well, that's not rocket science, either, Luke. I've known that since she sang 'Ave Maria' at the mass I went to."

"She sings 'Ave Maria'?"

"I just said so."

"I've never heard anyone sing that song except Mom-no ordinary person I mean. Of course, I've heard Celine Dion sing it but not anyone else that I knew personally."

"Neither had I, until three weeks ago."

"Oh, so you already noticed then."

"That she's a lot like Mom? Yes, Luke, I have."

Just then, the couple from the variety store approached us with greetings. I had met them the first night, but hadn't seen them since. They were friendly enough, but a little bizarre.

"We have the store just as you come into town. It's called the Village Idiot."

"Our motto is 'Your village called—their idiot is missing.'"

They had said this to me when I first met them. I didn't know what to say at that time and so had made no reply. Luke, it seemed was following suit.

"You are CFAs," the man continued.

"Pardon?"

"CFAs," his wife said, as if clearing up the matter.

"What does that stand for?" Luke asked.

"'Come from away.' That's what it stands for."

Quinn intervened at this time and tried to stabilize the conversation. Soon he and Luke were chatting about snowmobiling and ice fishing. When the store owners had moved on, Quinn said "They're all right, just a little different, that's all. No harm in them."

"They don't bother me," Luke said expansively. He half turned to me and winked discreetly. There was a thread of humor like quicksilver running through Luke. My dad had been like that, too.

There sure is a diversity of people living up here, I thought to myself as I looked around. I was starting to shiver, so I headed closer to the fire. Soon the music would be playing again, and no one would be cold once the dancing resumed.

Luke came over and stood beside me.

"Isn't it nice here?" I asked.

"I can't believe you, Gill. You're falling in love with this place."

"No, I'm not. Well, maybe a little. I can't help it. Life seems so wonderful here—so simple. I like it here. Maybe I will stay here. If anyone wants to find me, I'll be here."

"You're bewitched by this place, that's all. Maybe it's not as good as it seems."

"What do you mean?"

"Gillian," his voice was dead serious now. "Do you remember when we were kids and we used to watch Stephen King's *Tales from the Darkside?*"

"Kind of."

"They showed all these scenes along country roads, and then they said to every side of life, there is a dark side."

"That's just Stephen King. He believes in monsters and spirits too."

"I know that. But, Gilly . . ."

"Yes?"

"Somebody killed that boy."

27

I hated for my brother to leave. I hated to see him get in his truck and head south, out of Truman and back home. In spite of all my words to him about staying here, I knew that home for me would always be Newmarket and our funny little shop, where our mom had spent so many happy hours that it felt as if part of her were still there, steeped inside those walls. But I would always want to come back here. I wanted to stay in touch with Isabelle and Skylor, in particular. I wanted to make sure that Skylor used every scrap of that talent he had. It was a great gift to paint as he did. I didn't want it to go to waste.

Only one more week to spend up here. I couldn't believe it. I wanted to spend it with the Murfs and the Barnetts, drinking Earl Grey tea and sitting beside that magnificent fireplace, with the wildlife pokers and the delicious smell of lavender and cinnamon in the air. I wanted to snowshoe and do Girl Guide crafts and walk with the dogs, Truman and Jugs, and sleep well at night from so much fresh air and cold wind on my cheeks.

And that is what I did. I enjoyed every minute I had left. In some ways, I felt closer to Willie and Isabelle than I did to some of my friends back home. We had talked and laughed over so many things. I guess it's a little like the stranger that you meet on the train or subway: You know that he's not a part of your life, and so you can open up without any worries that it will come back to haunt you at a later date. I had discussed things very candidly with these women, and I think that they had done the same. I felt as if I knew them inside and out.

One night, I couldn't sleep for some reason. It wasn't very late—only about eleven o'clock—but I had been lying down for three-quarters of an hour and felt quite restless. I got up and dressed and went for a walk, slipping out the back way so as not to disturb Sadie and George. I imagined after spending a long day on their feet, they would have no problem drifting into dreamland.

I always caught my breath at the magnitude of that vast expanse of northern sky. It was one of those wonderful things that stayed with me—the clarity and brightness of the stars and the northern lights, which, it seemed, were never too far away.

I reflected that I would never do this at home. If I couldn't sleep at eleven o'clock, I'd probably turn the TV on to some old *Friends* reruns. I wouldn't don my winter garb and set out for a walk around the block. But I liked being out at night by myself; I had forgotten that. I had grown up and gotten cynical, but I remembered that as a small girl, I sat out on the front porch with my dad (who was always awake a little later, or so it seemed) to watch the show that consisted of the stars and the moon. I hadn't done it in years, but the feeling returned to me in a rush—the feelings of wonder and joy and humbleness from looking at the huge, other world that was the night sky.

The snow crunched underneath my feet, and I could feel my cheeks turning pink as the cold air found them under my hat and scarf. I felt utterly happy, as if life were quite simple and care-free. *I must remember this feeling. I must take this feeling home with me.* Mom used to say that all experiences were enlightening and to be learned from. If Luke and I had been disappointed or upset about circumstances that had taken place, she would say in her straightforward way, "Just chalk it up to experience and learn what you can from it."

If I was to learn anything from my Truman stint, it would be to stop and enjoy life, and sometimes take time to do the things that I enjoyed first. It was funny that I would have to come all the way up here to learn that, especially when I had initially been so reluctant to come. But the good ladies of Singing Pines had taught me that—and to snowshoe too.

As I walked past the Murphys' place and the sign with the Smurf in the green hat, as well as all the family members listed on it, I thought of the first time I'd seen it and how confused I'd been. Now I couldn't imagine not knowing them and their mother, who was the salt of the earth as far as I was concerned. I chuckled out loud as I remembered her talking about "Murphy's Law" when something went wrong, as it frequently did in a family of seven; and the other night, when she got her finger caught in the glue gun, she said, "Jesus Murphy!" and her husband's answer came from across the room: "Yes, Willie?"

They were like a family from another era. For one thing, I don't think that I knew any family at home with four children, let alone five. But I liked the way they operated. It made me wonder what it would be like to have more siblings. Nice, I thought, especially with Mom and Dad gone so young.

I glided silently by their house. It was totally dark, and the house itself seemed to be asleep. It looked big and cozy and peaceful.

I walked along and saw a light on in the upstairs room at Isabelle's. I could see her at her table, bending over and working away at some fabric. I stopped and looked at her for a little while, guessing that this was how she got so much work done. She probably made a practice of working into the night for a while after Skylor had gone to bed. She never mentioned it, and she never complained of fatigue when Willie and I arrived for our early-morning snowshoeing. But I had sometimes wondered how she managed to get everything done that she did, because I could see how her quilts progressed and how much time and effort she put into them. And I knew that she had some orders that she needed to finish for Christmas. She was a remarkable woman that was for sure.

I started when the wind rustled the dry leaves on the branches beside me. I hadn't realized that I had been standing there as long as I had. Suddenly, I felt guilty for watching her when she couldn't see me. I felt sneaky, even if I was watching her in admiration. I always found it a little unnerving that someone could look inside a lighted window from the outside darkness and watch people who were totally unaware that they were being observed. It seemed unfair, somehow. I turned and headed back to Sadie's and thought that I would be glad to crawl into that warm bed with the quilt that had been fashioned by Isabelle's fingers.

I would keep that night with me, though, remembering it — the feeling of it — for a long time. It was a good feeling, and I slept soundly after I sneaked inside and up the stairs to my nice warm room.

When Sadie called me for a phone call the next morning, I went downstairs eagerly, thinking that it was Luke calling. But it wasn't.

I'd forgotten (quite willingly) that Luke had said Sally might call and want to get together. But after I'd lifted the receiver, it was too late — I couldn't think of an excuse why I wouldn't be able to meet her for lunch the following Sunday. Damn!

28

For years and years to come, I was to ask myself over and over why on earth I ever agreed to drive to Cochrane to meet Sally Big Boobs on my last Sunday up north. I didn't want to, I dreaded the drive, and I was quite comfortable with all of the Singing Pines folks now. I wasn't lonely anymore and could hardly imagine that I'd ever felt lonely at all. I was actually starting to feel at home here in this remote, frozen land of ice and snow and song and fellowship. I could see myself returning to Truman Sound and gladly catching up on news of the Murfs and Isabelle and Skylor. I had to make myself get into my little blue jewel and head northeast on the highway.

If it wasn't for my brother, I never would have agreed to such a meeting. But he really wanted me to meet with her at least once during my stay. I'm quite sure that he thought it let him off the hook. And he thought that it was a great thing that she had recommended us for this job. I didn't see how. I hadn't made any great progress, and I told him as much on a regular basis. But he still insisted that it looked good for us to have been hired for such a job.

The upshot of the whole deal is that I found myself reluctantly and resentfully pulling into Cochrane at three o'clock to meet Sally in a dingy little bar off the main drag. Cochrane was a dull little town, its only claim to fame being the polar bears (which I did not visit this time), but I had learned my lesson about small towns. I remembered how I had felt when I first entered Truman and how desolate and isolated it had seemed. And it warmed my heart to think of how pleasant the time had become and how much I had enjoyed all of the time spent with my newfound friends.

Sally was already there, and I slid into a booth opposite her. She had a beer in front of her, and I got the impression it wasn't her first.

Oh great, I thought. *She's bad enough when she's cold sober.*

If anyone has ever watched *Corner Gas*, he will be able to visualize the dark little place where we met. It seemed to be an exact replica of the Dog River Inn, except here, a lot of people spoke French, both the staff and the patrons. They were friendly, though, and I accepted a beer. I thought it might make the tryst more bearable.

"I'm glad you could make it, Gillian," Sally said, slurring her words only very slightly. "I've been waiting."

"It's just three o'clock now," I stated mildly.

"Oh, I know, but I've been looking forward to seeing someone from my neck of the woods, so to speak. It gets pretty lonesome traveling around up here, going from place to place. You don't get to really know anyone. And nobody likes to see the social worker anyways. Usually I intervene only when there's trouble."

I immediately felt guilty for my earlier thoughts and for my reluctance. Sally was a flashy, forward kind of a girl, the type who tended to repel me. I was very down-to-earth, and she simply was not the sort of person whom I cared for. It hadn't occurred to me that she might be lonely or feel isolated. I was a little ashamed, and I tried to speak in a more kindly fashion.

"I never thought of it like that. It is pretty far from the GTA, isn't it? Why don't you get something a little closer to your family, if you feel that way?"

"There are no jobs available. You know, it's the same old story: It's hard to get a job without experience, and you can't get experience without a job."

I nodded in sympathy (I hoped).

"I was hoping maybe Coop would get in touch with me when he was up." She looked at me wistfully, and my feelings of camaraderie soon dissipated.

So this was the reason for her interest in me. It was as I suspected all along: she was just trying to weasel her way into my brother's affections. I could have told her that it was a losing battle and saved myself the two-hour trip.

"He was up for only one overnight, and it's a long way for that. He wasn't even going to come at all. He always thinks that he's indispensable at that security job he's taken on. He hates getting someone to cover for him, even for just one weekend."

"I know. He's very conscientious," she said a little thickly, taking another swig of her beer.

I rolled my eyes, but she didn't seem to notice.

"I actually thought that he'd take the whole assignment. I never dreamed he'd send his sister so far away."

I'm sure you did think he'd be the one sitting here now, I thought wryly, although these thoughts were just an echo of what my own had been.

The waiter brought my beer, and I took it gratefully. I realized that I hadn't drunk anything but Ale Murphy's homemade wine for weeks. This was cold and refreshing.

Sally ordered another, and I felt a little worry in the pit of my stomach. It was pretty early in the afternoon to be drinking so steadily. I was far from a prude, and I didn't really care what the next person was up to, especially one who was flaunting her wares as blatantly as Sally Big Boobs was, but I also didn't want her to get in an accident or anything.

As if reading my thoughts, she said, "I'm not driving, you know. I'm actually staying the night just across the road there."

"Oh, that's good."

"You're just like Coop. He'll have a drink, but he can't stand drinking and driving."

"I never said a word."

"Didn't have to. I could read it in your face."

"I'm sorry. Mom did drill that into our heads-Luke and mine I mean. It's hard to get past it."

"You always call him Luke, don't you?"

Oh great, we're getting maudlin now. "That's his name, Sally."

"At college, I didn't know that for the longest time. Everyone called him Coop."

I knew that his friends all called him Coop, but I had never gotten into that habit, probably because Mom always said that Lucas was the most beautiful name for a male that she ever knew. Apparently, it means "bringer of light," and Mom thought it was most appropriate. I never heard her say anything about the name Gillian.

The waiter came over with a pad and paper, and I ordered some fries and a hamburger, more to inspire Sally than out of a real feeling of hunger. I was afraid that if she kept drinking at this rate, that she would be passed out at the table soon, and then what would I do?

She took my lead and ordered the same. Then she started back on her favorite subject—my brother. I sighed. I loved my brother, but I didn't feel like listening to his praises sung for the entirety of a Sunday afternoon.

I managed to change the subject by asking about her acquaintance with Barbara Mainwright.

"Oh, for God's sake! I haven't even asked you how you're doing on your big case." She said this with not the slightest hint of sarcasm.

"Well, I don't know how much of a big case it is. I don't seem to have found out anything startling. The consensus of the whole town seems to be that he just fell and knocked his head out in the bush. I feel as if I'm grasping at straws."

She nodded and shrugged. She was starting to look a little bleary-eyed. I hoped that our food wouldn't take too long.

"I never thought that there was anything to the whole deal either, really. It's just that she was so adamant, you know."

"I know. I've talked to her a few times."

"It's too bad, really," Sally sighed deeply as she drained the last of her long-necked bottle. "Not that I think he was a nice kid, by any means."

I nodded. "The general opinion seems to be that he was full of himself and thought he was a real jock. That's not too uncommon in a sixteen-year-old boy who's too good-looking for his own good, though. Most of them get over themselves when they mature a little. Too bad Ryan never will never get the chance. I don't imagine there was too much real harm in him."

"I don't know." Sally was definitely slurring her words now. "There was that incident with the little Barnett boy—you know, the one who's a little slow. Did you meet him?"

"I did, actually. He told me that Ryan took his backpack once. I guess he was a bit of a bully."

She looked at me sideways and winked in a lewd fashion. "Took more than his backpack, I'll have you know, Miss Coop. Took his virginity too."

"What?"

"Shhh," she put her finger to her mouth in an exaggerated manner. "I shouldn't be telling you this. It's confidential, if you know what I mean."

Then don't tell me, I begged silently, while another part of me was listening avidly. I wish that I had gotten up and left right then and there, no matter how rude it was. But I didn't. I stayed and listened. And that was my undoing. Because words once said can never ever be unsaid.

"He raped him," she explained in a loud whisper which penetrated into my very soul. "Ryan did. He raped that funny little boy. You've met him, you say, so you know what he's like. He's a shy, lost thing. I heard that his mom did a lot of drugs when she was pregnant with him, and I think that it did something to his brain. I mean, he's just not right. Anyways, he lives with his grandmother, and she reported it, but she waited about a month after the incident. There wasn't much to be done then. It was too late, really. Ryan denied it, and there was no proof or anything. The grandma was very upset. They called me in to do some counseling, but the kid didn't say much at all. The kid—what's his name again?"

"Skylor," I said dully.

"Ya, Skylor. Well, he had been bleeding rectally, according to the grandma, and that's how she found out. The kid, Skylor, hadn't told her when it happened."

I felt as if someone had punched me right in the stomach, and I was reeling from the blow.

Our food came, and we went through the ritual of salt and vinegar and ketchup. I looked at the plate of food and wondered if I would be able to eat so much as a bite of it.

"Was Ryan a homosexual?" I asked quietly.

"Actually, that's one of the myths around sexual abuse of young boys. All men—I'm referring to Ryan as a man and Skylor as a boy, because that's the way it seemed to be—who sexually abuse boys are not necessarily homosexual. Lots of them are heterosexual, but aren't interested in fucking grown men. They're pedophiles, really. Most homosexuals aren't pedophiles."

She was eating now and seemed immediately to be clearer cognitively.

"Do you mean that Ryan was a pedophile?"

"It's quite possible. He wasn't really grown up himself, but he certainly viewed himself as a man."

"Oh, my God."

"I didn't mean to upset you, Gillian."

"I'm not upset," I lied and made a visible effort to take a bite of my burger.

She shrugged. "It's a terrible thing to say, but you do get used to this shit. After working in social work for a while, the surprise is when you find a normal family. They seem to be very few and far between, I'll tell you that much."

"I believe you."

"I'll tell you another thing," she waved a French fry at me for emphasis as she warmed to her topic. "Children with disabilities are four to ten times more vulnerable to sexual abuse."

"That's terrible," I whispered.

Sally nodded her agreement. "I'm telling you, it's a rough old world. You've met them though, you say. I guess they survived all right. Didn't have much choice, really, when all's said and done. I'll never forget it, though, because the grandmother was so upset. She looked as if she'd like to kill him. Who can blame her? But I guess it all turned out okay. All's well that ends well, right?"

29

When I was younger, Mom and I often had a jigsaw puzzle out on the dining room table, and we'd sometimes work on it in the evenings. We'd turn all of the pieces over and then systematically get all of the edge pieces together until we had the whole perimeter of the puzzle connected in a big rectangle. Then we would work away at the interior. Sometimes it took us weeks and weeks. And sometimes we would be stumped until we got one essential piece in the middle, and the rest would seem to fall into place. The picture was crystal clear.

That was how I felt at this moment. I thought of all the little pieces scattered about. I thought of those big, heavy pokers that adorned Isabelle's fireplace. I thought of the SOS signals that could be flashed so easily across a frozen expanse of river. I thought of Ryan Mainwright, who was a jock and a bully and now a molester of younger boys. I thought of an isolated spot in the woods and how a person could fall there from a heavy blow and not be found for hours and hours, and even then, be covered by a mantle of relentless white snow.

But most of all, I thought of Skylor—of his sweetness and how he blushed when someone complimented him, and how he loved his grandma and his friends, especially Fiona. And how broken he was when he came from British Columbia to a woman who knelt in a snow bank and held out her arms to him. And how he could run right into those arms because he knew, even as a neglected little boy, that now he could be safe and loved. Always. That his grandparents would do anything for that. Anything.

I felt ill right to the very core of my soul. I kept thinking that there must be a very reasonable explanation for all of these new thoughts. As soon as I talked to Isabelle, I was sure that she would laugh away the worry that was gnawing at my heart. She would pour me a mug of the Earl Grey tea that I had taken such a shine to and sit down with me by the fire and allay all of my anxieties. I felt as if I wanted to rush over just so that I could have that reassurance. But something held me back—something that felt like ice taking up residence deep inside of me.

Because why?—why?—why would Isabelle not have told me about the sexual attack on Skylor? She had not held information about him back from me. She had talked about his difficult beginning of life and other battles, which he had overcome with the help of his grandparents' love. It seemed so strange that she had never mentioned this incident especially when it involved the very subject that I was investigating i.e. Ryan Mainwright.

I reflected with anxious clarity on how absolutely neutral she had actually been on the whole subject of Ryan Mainwright. Even when the kids had been discussing how he had been a bit of a bully and teased the smaller ones, Isabelle had added no input of her own. I had thought at the time that she'd had no experience with this aspect of him. About that, at least, I was totally wrong.

I tossed and turned that night and replayed the scene with Sally over and over again in my head. I wished that I could just tell myself that she was lying, but I knew the truth when I heard it. It didn't stop me from hating her for it. The hate that I felt for her almost surpassed my worry. I knew that it was totally unreasonable, but I didn't care, not one bit.

If Luke had been privy to the tortures of my mind, he would have urged me "not to shoot the messenger," figuratively speaking. Again, I didn't care. I felt as if someone had reached inside of my heart and scooped out a big hollow spot. I realized that this was not exactly rational either, because I had known these folks for only five weeks. But to use a time-weary cliché, I had "bonded" with them in ways that tunneled deep inside of me. Isabelle, in particular, I felt close to.

Luke was right: I felt, in part, as if I had my mom back for this last little while. I couldn't bear to think what I was thinking. I wish that I could shut my brain off and let it rest. Perhaps it would function better after a rest. But that was not going to be my solace. I think it would be fair to say that I did not sleep at all, not one wink. I have heard people say that before, and I always thought that they were exaggerating, but I found out for myself that it is quite possible. And it doesn't make things look any brighter in the morning, either.

The morning sky dawned as grey and dull as my heart felt. I knew that Willie and Isabelle were going into Timmins to do some Christmas shopping that day, so I still had a bit of time to turn things around in my brain. They'd asked me to accompany them, and I had been looking forward to it, my first outing in weeks, but I simply could not go and pretend that everything was normal.

I knew Willie would be up before dawn because they were leaving early in order to get back home while there was still daylight. Willie had a big Girl Guides meeting planned for the evening, and Fiona and Skylor had agreed to assist since it involved fashioning Christmas decorations and Yule logs from evergreen boughs and birch bark logs. It sounded complicated to me, but I knew that Willie would take it in her stride, just like everything else. I also knew that Skylor was staying overnight at the Murfs'.

I knew this because I had become an integral part of their lives, and I knew all of their comings and goings. And I knew that I was going to have to go and see Isabelle. I had to talk to her. Tonight. Just the two of us. I had to get things straightened out, one way or the other, or I would go crazy, pure and simple.

It was my last day in Truman Sound. I was supposed to stay until the weekend, but somewhere in the clutches of that last night, which I had managed to survive, I realized that after I talked to Isabelle, I would have to leave. I couldn't stay for another Saturday of their festivities and gaiety. I just couldn't, unless I was way off in my surmising, and I didn't think that I was. I had a gut feeling that I was hoping against hope and was wrong.

I spent the day packing and filling my little "Honda Fart," as Luke would say, with all the accumulated possessions from my Truman Sound stay. There was a quilted throw from Isabelle, and a painting from Skylor that I had admired. There were several crafts from the Murfs—not just Guides ones, but some that they had initiated on their own.

I remembered how lonesome and homesick I had felt when I arrived, and I couldn't believe that I was feeling so bad about my departure. I wished that I had stayed as aloof as I had felt on my arrival. I wished that I had never gotten attached to any one at all up here. Especially Isabelle Barnett.

I ate a solitary supper at Sadie's. I'd even miss them, I thought, and then I acknowledged to myself that I was pathetic. I needed to get back to my own life without delay. I needed to be myself again.

I waved to Sadie as I left, and old Pete doffed his baseball cap at me. The only words I'd ever heard him say for five weeks were "bon jour," but he always acknowledged me with a tip of his hat. *At least he was who I knew him to be,* I thought bitterly, *not some imposter whom I had grown to actually love, only to find out that she was someone else altogether.*

I arrived at Isabelle's as the first blanket of early darkness fell over the land. The stars were so bright and clear that it hurt to look at them. I rapped on the door and pushed it open as she called out for me to come in. No one ever locked their doors up here. Why would they? Everyone knew everyone else. There was no crime, no worry about the unknown. I shivered to myself.

She was wiping off the kitchen table, when she saw me, her eyes lit up with an emotion that I knew to be genuine. That was what made it all so hard.

"Gillian! We missed you today. Willie and I both were hoping that you would have been able to come."

I bent over and removed my boots as she set out mugs and the big blue teapot that I had grown to associate with such warmth and friendship.

"I'm so glad that you came, dear. Skylor is staying up at the Murphys' tonight, and I was hoping for your company. I was thinking that maybe . . ."

She stopped in mid-sentence as she saw my face. "Gillian dear, what is it? What's the matter?"

For the umpteenth time since my arrival at Truman Sound, I was struck by her resemblance to my mother. I knew that was part of the reason why I felt so close to her. If I had been thinking in a reasonable manner, I wouldn't have done what I did next. I would have thought about it a little more before I opened my mouth, before I turned my anguished face to her and asked, in a strangled voice that didn't even sound like mine,

"Why didn't you tell me that Ryan Mainwright sexually abused and assaulted Skylor? Did you think that it had no bearing on what I was here for?"

30

Isabelle looked at me and sighed deeply.

Here it is, I thought. *Here is your chance to tell me that it has nothing to do with the case at all. That the abuse was just a horrible episode that occurred and was now over and done with.* I was silently begging her to set me free of this whole anxiety, but I knew in my heart that it was too late for that, way too late.

"Sit down," she said in a hollow voice.

She slowly put the mugs away and got out two wine glasses. "We may need a little help with this. And Skylor isn't coming home."

She proceeded to produce a wine bottle and poured a generous portion into each respective glass.

"I suppose it was that Sally Wamless who told you. It must have been. No one else in the world knew, I'm almost certain."

A part of my brain was surprised to learn that Sally Big Boobs actually had a surname. I was quite sure that I had never heard it before. She would always be Sally Big Boobs to me. *I wish that I never had known her* was my next, bitter thought.

I sighed and nodded my head in silent agreement.

Isabelle sighed too and sat down heavily in the kitchen chair across from me.

"What is the use of being a professional if you take peoples' private lives and gossip about them in the local watering holes? I thought that these people were supposed to have a high standard of confidentiality, like lawyers or something."

I shook my head miserably. "I don't know. I wished that she'd never told me. I didn't ask her, Isabelle. She's just always trying to stay in touch with my brother, and so I think that she thinks she can sidle her way into my life. I wish that she'd never told me," I repeated.

"I wish that it never happened," Isabelle said simply. "But it did, and we've had to go on. It was right after Reg died, and Skylor and I were both struggling. That's the way bullies are, you know. They kick you when you're already down. And Skylor is fragile at the best of times. We survived it, though, Gillian. I never told another living soul. Not even Willie knows. I'm sorry that you found out."

I took a gulp of the sweet, clear wine and said in a low voice, without looking at Isabelle, "I am upset because I didn't know about the abuse before, and that it might have made a difference at how I looked at everything."

"What do you mean?"

"Well," I forged ahead with the words that I had been rehearsing for almost twenty-four hours, with my voice low and my head bowed, "I kept going over and over in my mind that there was no motive. I kept saying this when I spoke to Barbara Mainwright, and it was reiterated by everyone whom I spoke to. What possible motive could anyone have for killing a sixteen-year-old boy? I mean, by all accounts, he was a bit of a conceited kid—full of himself—but you don't get murdered for that. I didn't realize that he had hurt someone so badly, so badly that a person might actually want to kill him."

Isabelle was absolutely still. She could have been a statue. She didn't look at me. This gave me the courage to go on.

"I felt sick to my stomach when I found out what happened to Skylor at Ryan's hands. I can only imagine how you must have felt. I know how much you love him. I think that you were okay with things for a while. Well maybe not okay, but I think that you came to terms with it all. I think that you survived until Ryan started hanging around Singing Pines."

She looked up at me sharply, but said not a word, either in denial or affirmation.

"I think that Ryan was coming around, and you thought that it was just a matter of time before he struck again. Sally confirmed that, actually. She thought that he was a bully and would probably remain one. I think that you saw him hanging around on Halloween night and knew that he was up to no good. Barbara Mainwright always makes him sound like a perfect angel, and no one ever really contradicted that—not even you or Skylor—so I never thought that his intentions would have been so evil. I thought he was just a teenager out and about on Halloween night. Maybe he'd had a beer or two, but there was no harm to anyone. That wasn't the case though was it, Isabelle? He was up to a lot of harm."

Again, Isabelle looked up with a wary expression, but said nothing. She looked completely defeated, and I felt terrible that I was the cause of that defeat.

"I think that it wasn't the first time you'd seen him around. You may have even warned him. But by this time, you knew how useless the police were in the case of a young offender. And so did Ryan. I think that you decided to take matters into your own hands. I think that you flashed that old SOS signal at Quinn, and he came over to help you. I think that's why he stayed the night before your surgery. It didn't have anything to do with your worry over the operation. I should have known that was a crock right from the beginning. He came over to help you and give you an alibi. And it would be plausible, too, because no one would question the Mighty Quinn. He's too well thought of around here."

"Gillian, please leave Quinn out of this. He didn't have anything to do with anything. Please, Gillian, you have to believe me about this."

I went on as if I hadn't heard her. I had to get it all out before it gnawed a great big hole inside of me. "I think that you saw him out there, and it was the last straw for you. Skylor was at the Murphys', and you were going to Timmins the very first thing in the morning. I think that you took one of those big, heavy, handmade pokers that you keep by the fire, and you went after him. He wouldn't be afraid of you by any means, especially if he had alcohol on board. He already knew he could get to you, as he'd done before. Maybe he even taunted you with that. I don't know. And maybe you just meant to scare him. I don't know that either. But I think that you took that poker and smashed the base of his skull in with it. And it killed him. I'm just speculating, mind you. But a blow, like he had, to the back of the head could have been made by a big rock, I would imagine"

The words filled the kitchen like a living thing and lay between us as we silently sipped our wine. I felt as if I might need another bottle or two to make it through this night.

After a long pause, I continued in my surmising.

"I think that it scared the shit out of you, and that's when you signaled to Quinn. I think that you cleaned the poker off and probably burned it in the fire for a while to remove any traces of anything if anyone came looking. But why would they? And it snowed that night too. Quite a bit, as it does up here. Ryan wasn't found until well into the next day, and everything was covered in snow by then. And you were long-gone to the hospital, with your foot in a cast and staying overnight because of the worry about your heart. Quinn could attest to that fact. I remember that you told me once that a good loyal friend was by far better that a lover."

I wanted her to deny it all. I wanted her to tell me that I had been watching too many mysteries on TV and listening to too much Agatha Christie. But she didn't. Part of me wished that she would even lie. I thought that if she lied, I would do my utmost to believe her. Again, she didn't.

She took her glass over to the counter and set it down very deliberately. The she turned and looked at me. When she did, I felt as if I were looking straight into her soul. I felt as if I could see the icy depths of her that were capable of great hate—and great love. And I didn't know which was worse.

I almost didn't recognize her voice or her face as she said, never taking her eyes off of mine, "Gillian, you know Skylor, don't you? You know him pretty well, I think."

"Yes. He's a great kid."

"In what world—in what world and by what standards— would anyone think that it would be acceptable to let a child like that suffer as he has? A beautiful, precious boy who never hurt anyone in his whole life? In what world would he have to be born a crack baby and live in squalor for the first two years of his life, and then, at the age of thirteen, be bum-fucked by the class bully?"

31

I was shocked. Even in the context of our conversation, I was shocked by her language. I'd never heard Isabelle say anything more profane than "damned," and what she just said sounded like a foreign language on her tongue and to my ears.

She brought the wine bottle over and sloshed some more wine in both of the glasses. I didn't care. It was going to be a long night.

She seemed to realize the effect her words had on me. I'm sure they sounded strange to her as well. "I'm sorry," she said simply.

But I noticed that she didn't deny any of it, as I was longing for her to do. I thought about this. I thought about the fact that if she was a cold-blooded murderer, that I was alone with her, and that she had a motive to kill me too. But I wasn't the least bit afraid. I was quite certain that Isabelle Barnett would not hurt me. In fact, I felt that she loved me. And as I thought all of this, it came to me with awful clarity that I must be right—that she had killed Ryan. But I also knew that she would never have done it if Ryan hadn't posed such a threat to her beloved boy. She was protecting her young. Did that justify murder, though? I didn't know anything anymore.

"I'm sorry, Gillian," she repeated.

"It's not me that you have to be sorry to. What about the Mainwrights? What am I supposed to tell them?"

"I don't know. I don't know." Her voice was miserable, and her words were almost a moan. "Do you think I haven't thought of him every minute of the day for the last year? I'm supposed to be a Christian. And while I have never thought that makes me better than others, I have tried to live in the hopes that I can be a good person."

I looked unconsciously at the sign on her kitchen window sill, which was her only concession to any religious references. It displayed the golden rule: "Do unto others as you would have others do onto you."

"He was their only child," I said softly. "They're all alone now."

"A child who would grow up to be a sadist—an abuser, or worse." Her tone was angry now. "This wasn't just a school prank, Gilly, or a weak kid getting picked on. Skylor was damaged physically for a long time. He had internal lacerations, and he bled for days-not to mention what he went through mentally. It was just horrible"

"If you knew, why didn't you do something right away? Sally says that you didn't report it for a month, and that it was almost an afterthought."

"He didn't tell me. I knew something was wrong, of course, because he's usually such a happy boy. I mean, I know that Skylor has limitations and that he will probably always be a little behind. But you've seen him. He has a great life here. He's pals with the Murphys, especially Fiona. He fits in there; they accept him for who he is. He's back to who he was before it all happened, thank God. I don't want him to ever be that boy again—

that abused, withdrawn boy. I probably would never have found out if it wasn't for his paintings. You've seen his paintings, Gillian. He can create life with his hands and brush."

"I think he's a genius." And I meant it.

"Well, it's true that a picture is worth a thousand words. I got the message pretty clearly when I found the painting of the episode with Ryan. Of course, I didn't know it was Ryan, but by then Skylor was ready to tell me, I think. Not to mention the fact that he needed new underwear. All of his were stained with blood by that time. But. I'll never forget how I felt when I saw that painting and I put all of the pieces together. Skylor just wept and wept when he told me. It broke my heart. You know they always talk about girls being raped, but it is just as devastating for a young boy. And they are so ashamed. Anyways, it was over a month after the incident, but I didn't ignore it, you know. I actually went to the local police. I didn't even go to the school. I wanted to show Skylor that we needed to do things through the proper channels. Barbara Mainwright is right about one thing, anyways. The cops around here are not too ambitious. Of course, the one who saw us isn't even here anymore. That was his last year here, and now he lives in Florida, I think. But the guys here now aren't much better."

That's why they didn't make any connection either, I thought, *when Ryan was killed so close to the Barnetts'. It's pretty bad if I could make a connection like that.* Of course, I knew Isabelle and how deep her love for Skylor flowed within her. And I hadn't known all of the facts until Sally spilled out her guts to me.

"There's not much they can do anyways," Isabelle continued bitterly. "Skylor was just thirteen and not that great under pressure. I know that he would never lie. That's not who he is. But I guess every parent and grandparent says that. And Ryan came off smelling like a rose. Money can buy a lot, you know. I never believed that. I never wanted to believe that, but it's true. And it's a shame that young offenders are so protected because, as far as I'm concerned, if someone does something really evil like that when they're young, then that's who they are. They're never going to change."

I had no idea what to say. I looked at her with defeated, miserable eyes. "Oh, Isabelle, Isabelle, why couldn't you have just lied to me?" I asked mournfully.

She leaned forward in her chair and placed a tentative hand on mine.

"Gillian, sometimes people have a chance in their lives to do something really big, something that will make a difference in another's whole life. For myself, I don't care. I really don't. I'm sixty-six years old. I've lost the love of my life, and my children are far away. But for Skylor's sake, I am begging you to think of us. I'm the end of the road for him. I'm it. I'm all he's got between me and the rest of the world. His mother is lost in her drug-infested shell, and God only knows who his father is. I'm all he's got."

"He's got the Murphys. And Quinn."

"If they put me away, he'd go into care," she went on as if I hadn't spoken. "He'd get lost. This is your chance, Gillian, your chance to make a difference—a world of difference—to us. To Skylor and me. This is your chance to let us keep our lives. Skylor needs your mercy. Don't think about me at all. Just think of him.'

"The quality of mercy is not strained." The words wandered out of my mouth. I felt totally lost.

"It droppeth as the gentle rain from heaven," Isabelle picked up the thread of my words.

"I know my Shakespeare, Gillian. Do you know what that quote means?"

"It means that mercy cannot be strained, which is a word that used to mean 'forced.' We can't force it. We must …," my voice dropped to a whisper, "we must find it in ourselves."

"Yes, if we can."

The log cabin was quiet now. Only our breathing could be heard in the still, dim kitchen.

I sipped at my wine and did not trust myself to look at Isabelle or speak to her.

After a little while, Isabelle seemed to gain a little more of her usual composure. "Your friend Hercule Poirot would be very proud of you, my dear. You used your little grey cells and solved a case that had been given up on a year ago."

"My friend Hercule Poirot," I replied looking up at her with a sideways gaze, "does not approve of murder."

"That is true."

"Under any circumstances." I was warming to the topic. At least this was something that was cut-and-dried. "That is his recurring mantra through all of his books. He says it over and over. 'I do not approve of murder.'"

"Yes. I've read enough Christie to know that to be true. Except . . ."

"Except what?"

"Well, didn't you tell me that you're listening to *Murder on the Orient Express* on CDs in your car now? That you've listened to it lots of times before as well?"

"Yes," I admitted, knowing precisely where this conversation was going, as will any of you who are familiar with the story line.

"I thought that in that particular one, Poirot did let the murderers go free."

"Sort of. He agreed not to put the case forward to the authorities."

"Because the victim had been a child molester."

"Not exactly. He kidnapped the little girl and killed her. The people who murdered the man had all been in the little girl's life and they got together and killed him in turn. Skylor is still very much alive."

"How many attacks like the one he had at Ryan's hands do you think that he could survive? I try so hard, but I can't be with him every second of the day and night. He's fifteen."

I looked at her, and I could feel her grief and her love for her boy emitting from her as if it were a tangible thing. I felt completely and utterly horrible.

I got up and silently placed my glass in the sink. I knew that I would never again enter this sweet kitchen where I had spent so many warm, happy hours, and I could hardly bear it.

She stood up, too, and looked at me expectantly. She caught my hand as I walked by her and looked deep into my eyes.

"Of course," she said in a calm, quiet voice, "you must do what you think is best."

I hugged her fiercely, and when I pulled away, it was me who was crying. Her face was weary and sad, but her eyes were dry. I put my head down on her shoulder and sobbed as if my heart were breaking.

32

I turned away from the log cabin and stumbled out into the frigid, northern night. I would never see this magnificent sky again. It just wasn't the same in Newmarket. Nothing was the same. I had grown to love it up here, something that I would have thought unimaginable only a few short weeks ago.

As I passed the Murfs', it occurred to me that I should say good-bye to them as well. I had been so wrapped up in my mental turmoil that I wasn't thinking of anything else. And the Murphys had all been so hospitable to me. I couldn't just leave without a word. I was leaving at the first light of day, and then I would decide what to do. I was too close to it all here. I couldn't think straight. I had to get away. The thought consumed my mind. I had to leave. It took every ounce of will power I possessed to turn and head up the lane, past the green-capped Murf sign, and enter into the busy, noisy house.

It was hard, oh, so hard. They were all happy to see me, especially Skylor. The whole kitchen was filled with evergreen boughs, as if I had accidentally happened into the middle of a forest. This was accentuated by the birch logs that peppered the floor. The atmosphere was one of laughter and good times.

"Gillian! Is something wrong?"

I forced a smile onto my lips and tried to make my voice normal. "No, Willie. I'm fine. I just stopped to say good-bye. I'll be leaving first thing in the morning."

"Really? I thought that you weren't leaving until the weekend. I thought we had a few more days to enjoy your company."

Her words were commonplace enough, but her tone was wary. I knew that I looked upset, so I tried harder. Maybe she would just think that I was upset to leave Truman Sound. If that were the sum total of my upset, it could be remedied so easily. I could come and visit.

Her next words echoed my sentiments. "You'll just have to come and visit, Gill. It's not that far, really. It's so nice here in the summer. You've no idea."

I didn't want to see Truman in the summer. To me, Truman Sound was and always would be a winter town, a frozen, endless land of snow and ice and stars.

"I'll have to see what I can do, Willie. I want to thank you and Ale for all of your hospitality. You guys are about the nicest people I've ever known. I will never forget my weeks here. I've got some wonderful memories." My voice sounded a little strangled at the last words. I knew full well which memory would be the predominant one from Truman. Willie, though, was blissfully ignorant.

She put her arms around me and hugged me warmly. "We've loved every minute that we've spent with you, dear."

And the thought occurred to me that the first time and the last time that I was to see Willie Murphy, I had tears on my cheeks.

Skylor was kneeling down with Fiona, bending evergreen boughs into some fashion of a circle. They both grinned when they saw me. Skylor stuck his head through the circle and wagged his tongue at me. They both dissolved into laughter.

I was glad that the whole brood was there. It made it easier to be casual and airy, with promises to stay in touch. Skylor and Fiona both hugged me, and I felt bad to leave this way. Willie was still looking at me askance, as if she knew there was something else at the root of my story. She just wasn't sure what.

She insisted on writing down her email and her snail mail addresses for me, and she sent me on my way with a Ziploc bag full of cookies. I protested that I would dint her supply of Christmas baked goods, but she wanted me to have something for the ride home. She reminded me of the long, lonely miles ahead, with very little civilization to relieve it. I could barely face the thought of that drive, but I couldn't bear the thought of staying here another day.

The kids stood at the window and waved at me, and I waved back until I was swallowed up in the shadow of the huge branches of the pine trees. Then I let the tears stream unchecked down my cheeks, and what a relief it was. It was with a heavy, heavy heart that I turned down the street, passed the two churches, and turned right to Sadie's. I slipped in the back door so that I could enter my room without encountering anyone.

My mind was reeling, and my heart was aching. Part of me had been so firmly convinced that Isabelle would have a logical explanation for the whole incident. And I had so wanted to hear that explanation. I had longed for it. But of course, it had never been forthcoming because that other possibility, the one I couldn't bear thinking about, had come true. And I was totally devastated.

I didn't even go down for dinner that evening. I was too afraid that I would sit and weep into my meal. I wanted so badly to talk to someone. But the person that I wanted to talk to was Isabelle— or Willie. The former was unthinkable; the latter, impossible.

I ended up calling Luke to let him know that I would be traveling tomorrow and would try to be home by nightfall. He, too, was surprised by my abrupt homecoming, but he was satisfied that I had given it the "old college try."

"Are you okay, Gilly? You sound kind of tired or something."

I sighed deeply. "I'm all right. Just a little homesick, I guess. I've been here quite awhile, you know. I came the first of November and its December fourth tomorrow. I think I've fulfilled my duty." I was aware that my tone was getting sharper, and I let it happen. It was better than sobbing on the receiver.

"Hey, don't get your shirt in a knot."

That did make me smile because that was my mom's expression.

"I was just asking. You sound tired, that's all. Better get a good sleep tonight, Gill. It's a long, wicked drive. Anyways," his tone was lighter, "I've missed you here. Everyone's asking about you, and we've got a few new jobs. Somebody wants us to help put her Christmas lights up."

"Not exactly a detective job, is it?"

"Of course not. She saw the sign—you know, 'no job too small'—and she said it was worth a try to see if we'd help her. What do you think?"

"I think it's great. I'm sick of nosing around, asking the same questions over and over, and getting nowhere at all."

"So it's okay to take the job?"

"It's okay with me, Luke. Beggars can't be choosers, after all. We can't afford to turn down work."

"I agree. Anyways, do you want me to call the Mainwrights and tell them that you're done and you'll talk to them when you get home?"

"Go ahead. It's easier for you to call."

"Okay, I will. Be careful in that silly little blue fart. You could get lost among all those transport trucks. They might not even see you. Anyways, it'll be good to have you back."

"I can hardly wait," I said the words softly, and I just managed to keep the tears back as I rang off.

33

I slept a little better just knowing that my business here was completed and I had no more confrontations in store for me. I could go home. I hadn't been homesick for quite a while. I had thoroughly enjoyed my time here, but now that I knew my departure was imminent, I could hardly contain myself. I needed to do some serious soul-searching. I couldn't even think straight. I was too close to everything here.

I loaded my little blue Honda, and bracing myself, I went back into Sadie's for one last breakfast. They were busy this morning. There were a lot of ice fishermen in town, and Sadie and George were both running to keep up with the demands for coffee and homemade breakfast items. I imagined that most of these fellows were returning customers. They knew a good thing when they found it.

The Little Brown Jug came and sat beside my chair. I knew that Sadie didn't allow him in here as a rule, but she was too busy to notice, and he seemed to sense that this was my last meal here, or at least I liked to think that he did. I stroked his fat brown head. *I have grown fond of even him,* I sighed to myself.

As I lingered over my coffee, waiting for the light of day to brighten the world up just a little more before I braced myself for the journey south, I was surprised to see old Pete get up from his perpetual post at the window table and approach me.

He doffed his cap and said "bon jour," just as he had greeted me every morning for the past four and a half weeks.

I smiled and murmured a greeting in return, expecting him to pass by me without further comment, as was his wont. He surprised me, however, by asking me if I would be on my way today. His words and tone were quite polite and almost refined, not what I would have expected, if I'd thought about it.

"Yes, I'm heading home. I'll be glad to get home. I've been here long enough."

"I expect you have, ma belle. You're young. It's hard to understand things sometimes."

I looked at him curiously.

"What do you mean?"

"I just mean that blood is thicker than water, that's all. Have you heard that expression?"

"Yes. I know what it means. But I'm not sure what it has to do with anything."

His eyes pierced into mine as he said in an intense undertone, "It just means that blood is thicker than water and always will be. I haven't seen my family in many, many years. I have a grandson, and I wouldn't know him if he walked into this place right now. But I'll tell you one thing . . ."

"What's that?" I whispered, my heart beating wildly in my chest.

"If I knew that someone had hurt him—beat him or abused him or anything like that—I'd kill them, so I would."

He tipped his cap again and turned to walk nonchalantly out the back door of the restaurant.

I was absolutely stunned. If I hadn't been so astonished and upset, I would have laughed right out loud. Here I was, interviewing and exploring for all these days, and old Pete had known the answer all along. Not only did he know it, but apparently he condoned it. I felt like Alice in Wonderland. I felt as if everything were topsy-turvy. How Pete had acquired his information, I was never to know. I remembered Claude Maindiaux saying that he walked a lot, all over town. And I suspected that Pete was one of those people whom others overlooked, that he was essentially invisible in many ways because he didn't talk much or socialize. I hadn't thought that he would have been capable of the verbal exchange that we had just had. I wondered why he had bothered when I was on my way home. Maybe he just wanted to let me know that he knew. It must be lonely being him.

Sadie and George both hugged me fiercely and made me absolutely promise to return, to keep in touch, and to tell people about their place if they wanted a northern getaway. I promised all of these things, and I told them that I would miss them. I meant it. They had treated me so well. It wasn't only the meals. It was everything about them.

Sadie pushed a travel mug into my mittened hand. It was nice and warm, and the logo "Sadie's" was written in red across it. "That'll keep you warm for the way home. And you'll think of us whenever you use it."

She leaned forward and whispered conspiratorially, "There's a little bit of Baileys in it, Gillian love."

When I started to protest, she waved away my words and kissed my cheek.

"It'll keep you going, and that's no lie. I can see that you're getting awful homesick. It's getting close to Christmas, and folk do get homesick this time of year. You drive real safe, and you'll be home before you know it."

I gathered everything up, and as I was exiting the door, I turned for a final wave good-bye. Sadie and George were standing arm-in-arm, and as I left, they both waved. I heard their last word follow me out on the cold Truman wind. It was an echo of the apple lady from Haileybury a few weeks before, only it seemed like a life time ago.

"Godspeed."

34

I wanted to go home, but in some ways, what I wanted more than anything was to head down Singing Pines and hash everything over with Willie and Isabelle. They would be having their morning Earl Grey, and then they'd be heading out on their snowshoes for their self-imposed hour of exercise. I should be with them, should be laughing and chatting and gossiping with them. I would never be with them again.

I drove past the Newfie garage, and Shane and Ian waved as I tooted the horn and put my blinker on to retrace my route back home, heading south down Highway 11. I didn't listen to my audio mystery story. I didn't attempt to find a radio station. It was just me in the car, me and all of my newfound facts chasing themselves around and around in my head.

I was missing my mom. I wished that I could just talk things over with my mom. My mom had been the kindest, most loving woman in the whole world, and there was nothing in her that would condone murder. But it seemed as if none of this was black and white. I wondered what my mom would have done if someone had raped and beaten Luke when he was a young, helpless boy. I couldn't imagine. My mom and I had been friends. I loved her dearly. We shopped and talked and went on outings together. And I knew that she loved me too. But Luke was her boy. Luke was her shining star.

The day was steel-cold, and the sky was that bleak grey that seems to go on and on forever. I couldn't imagine that the sun would ever shine again. My heart felt like a dull, heavy lump lying in my chest.

And what to do? What to do? What to do?

There was nothing in my life that had equipped me to handle an event of this magnitude. I had always had quite a straightforward life. Certainly, I had always known right from wrong without any difficulty. But this situation, to me, was unimaginable. I knew that when I got home, Luke was going to make me write some sort of report for the Mainwrights, and rightly so. They did not pay two hundred dollars a day for the past five weeks to not get some accountability, even if their son was some type of a monster.

I shook my head. I was not supposed to know that. If I knew that, then as day follows night, I must know other things. And I didn't want to know the other things. I didn't want to. I wanted to be blissfully ignorant. I had to get away from this cold `place and be myself again. And I had to figure out what I was going to do. But not now. I would allow myself a week to get myself in order.

This immediately gave my mind relief, and I relaxed a little. I turned on my CD and listened for some time. I loved these mysteries. Usually I found them quite soothing. I would get lost in the old English way of storytelling. Of course, I had forgotten the plot of the present one during the intervening weeks, so

I ended up switching it off. I knew the story line of this one too well. I couldn't bear to hear all the witnesses talking about the evil Cassidy, who had kidnapped and killed little Daisy Armstrong. I knew it was a totally different situation from the one that Isabelle had faced, but I also knew that if Ryan had begun hanging about again, that perhaps her fears had been justified. Certainly, his intentions had not been honorable.

I drove and drove and drove, and that in itself was a sort of therapy. I was leaving the town farther and farther behind. And my earlier decision to give myself a week to get myself in order also helped lessen the anxiety. I was starting to breathe easier. I was going home.

I sighed to myself as I passed the cutoff for Haileybury. At one point, I had toyed with the idea of stopping and visiting again the beautiful statue that had touched me so deeply. But there wasn't enough distance from Truman yet. I couldn't stop. And the world up here was, oh, so cold and lonely.

I thought about my sweet little apple lady who had filled me in on the fire history and told me stories about the town. I didn't even know her name, but I would always remember her fondly. I wondered if she, too, hid some secrets deep in her soul. Maybe no one was as they seemed. I shook my head and forced myself to get to the state of semi-calm that I had achieved earlier. It was hard, but I had no choice. There was no one to share the whole story with, at least not until I figured out what I was going to do.

Hours and hours later, when the sun was starting to make its decline to the other side of the world, I finally stopped for fuel for my little Fit and for myself. I took the exit to Gravenhurst and felt I was finally getting near the end of the journey. I knew this area a little because of our old cottage in Bracebridge. At least it was somewhat familiar. And I was closer to home than I was to Truman Sound. If I could just hold on tight and keep body and soul together, I would arrive in Newmarket before dark.

I stopped on the main street of Gravenhurst and entered Sloan's Restaurant. It had been there a long time, I knew, and the building felt cozy and warm. The waitress who served me was in her fifties or so, and she was friendly, chatting about all the snow and that Christmas was coming and it would be here before we knew it. At this point, I couldn't quite bear the thought of Christmas. I could only just concentrate on getting farther south, to my beloved Newmarket. I felt as if I'd had enough winter to last the rest of the season. And it wasn't even Christmas.

After I had consumed a coffee and a grilled cheese with fries, I felt almost human again—in body, anyways.

The friendly waitress approached me with a fresh pot of coffee, but I declined. "I have to get back on the road," I explained.

"I can put it in a cup to go for you, if you like," she offered.

I remembered the travel mug that Sadie had given me, the contents of which were long gone, and thought that I could transfer it to that in the car. I could use more coffee. I still had another couple of hours to go.

The waitress was already returning with a large cardboard cup filled with coffee and a couple of gingerbread men wrapped up in a napkin. "No charge," she said cheerfully. "I was baking these with my grandchildren, and I brought the leftovers in."

"Thank you so much. You're very kind."

"No problem at all. Are you okay there, my dear? To drive I mean? You look a little tired."

"Oh, I'm fine. I'm on my way home. When I get there, I'll be fine. I've got some miles to go yet."

"Miles to go before you sleep."

I smiled at her, thanked her again, and headed to my car. Her words echoed in my head as I passed the little towns that I knew and recognized: Orillia, Barrie, Bradford, the Holland Marsh. As I passed each one, I felt better and better. When I finally got to the cutoff for Highway 9, which heads into Newmarket, there was hardly any snow at all. It didn't seem like winter had even come yet, not like in Truman Sound. I thought that it would be winter there forever. I was weary from the top of my head to the tips of my toes.

"And miles to go before I sleep."

35

I stepped into my old life and pulled my old familiar ways around me like a well-worn, comfortable sweater. I reveled in it. When I had finally pulled into my driveway on that evening of my long trip home, I had put my head down on the steering wheel and cried and cried from the sheer relief of being home.

It was easier to see things here. I became me again.

I'd called Luke to tell him that I was home. He said it was really quite busy and asked if I was okay to start working the very next day if I slept in a little bit. I was more than okay. I was ready and willing to start headlong into my old job. Simple, mindless chores would last me just fine for some time to come, I was sure. I did not want any more soul-searching cases for now.

After my self-imposed week of trying to abstain from thinking about Isabelle, I sat down to write something up for the

Mainwrights. In the report, I told them that I felt as if I'd wasted their money for five weeks; I had talked to most of the Truman folks over and over again, but that I really hadn't unearthed any information that was significant in their son's death. I was truly sorry that he had died so young and so needlessly.

And that was my decision. I really had no proof against Isabelle. If it came right down to it, it would be her word against mine. I had no concrete proof, although she had all but confessed. Yet, somehow, I knew that if it ever did come to anything, Isabelle would not deny the truth. That was not who she was. She was not a liar. I appreciated the awful irony of that. She may be a murderer, but she was not a liar.

The whole truth of the matter was that at the end of the day, I couldn't do it. I just couldn't. To this day, I don't know if that makes me a really compassionate person or the worst kind of a coward. It didn't matter. It didn't change anything. I was to be forever burdened with the knowledge. That's what I was left with.

If only my mom were living, I could have had some release. I could have talked it over with her. There was no one else to trust it with. It was too big and all encompassing. Maybe someday I would be able to tell Luke. Maybe not.

I never went back to Truman Sound, but I thought of it a lot. And sometimes I even longed to be there—the old way, the way it was before I knew what I knew now. I laughed to myself when I pictured the people out on the river, drinking homemade wine and dancing to "Truman Sound Saturday Night." And even now, the hint of a scent of cinnamon or lavender can transport me to that log cabin where I spent so many happy moments.

But Truman would always be to me a little like that town in Scotland that you can never find and where people get lost. I watched the old movie with Mom one time—*Brigadoon*, I think it was called. That's how Truman seemed to me: as if you could drive up that road and search and search and never find it. Maybe only once in a hundred years or so.

We never heard from Sally Big Boobs—or Sally Shit Disturber, as I called her in my own mind now. Luke heard through the grapevine that she had taken up with a fellow from Sault Ste Marie and they had moved out to British Columbia. This suited me right down to the ground. And I knew that it must have brought Isabelle some degree of peace of mind as well.

Isabelle. The thought of her still stirred my heart. I had grown to love her and Skylor so much. Maybe Luke was right, and part of me was looking for a mom again. But I liked her too. I enjoyed her company and her crafts and the way she looked at life. I admired her as a person. And I admired who she was to Skylor. They were, in one way or another, to haunt me for the rest of my days, even though I never laid eyes on either one of them again. But not one single day ever went by that I didn't think of them.

During my first days at home, I would go over it and over it in my mind until I thought I'd go crazy. It was easier to do nothing about what I'd learned, of course it was. I knew that. But was that the right thing to do, just because it was easier? I knew it wasn't legally, but what about morally? How could I do anything to uproot that sweet, fragile boy-child?

But was it enough? Was it enough to just let it be? Let it be forever?

And then I allowed myself to think about them. About the log house at the end of Singing Pines, with the inukshuk whose hat changed to suit various occasions, and the post with four bird houses and all the suet and feeders, and white and blue lights following the path down to the river. I thought about the train whistle and Skylor's face when he heard it. I thought of his beautiful paintings in that upstairs room, and the quilts and scrapbooks and photos and all the memories stored there. I thought of Skylor growing up safe and free with the Murfs and Quinn—and Isabelle.

And it was enough.

THE END

LaVergne, TN USA
02 February 2011
214843LV00001BA/1/P